BOOT TRACKS

Matthew F. Jones

BOOT TRACKS

Europa
editions

Europa Editions
116 East 16th Street
12th floor
New York, N.Y. 10003
www.europaeditions.com
info@europaeditions.com

Library of Congress Cataloging in Publication Data is available
ISBN 1-933372-11-7

Jones, Matthew F.
Boot Tracks

Book design by Emanuele Ragnisco
www.mekkanografici.com

Printed in Italy
Arti Grafiche La Moderna – Rome

*For all the old
souls in my life*

PART ONE

R ankin walked into the place and over to the desk. He
asked the little bitty Mexican-or-Indian-looking guy at
it if he knew Billy.

"Billy who?"

"Billy."

"I ain't sure if I do." Two silver teeth at the front of the guy's
mouth caught the light as he talked around a half-a-thumb-
length cigarette. "What's he look like?"

"Like Billy."

"Who's asking if I do?"

Rankin said his name.

"Figure this snow'll amount to anything, Charlie?"

Rankin didn't say what he figured.

"I don't either. And I've spent my whole life here."

Rankin couldn't tell if the guy was busting chops or was
making lame conversation; he didn't like it, anyway, him jerking Rankin around on the Billy thing (What's he look like?, for
Chrissake) instead of giving a flat-out yes like he'd been supposed to. A fake gold tag on the guy's lapel labeled him Ornay
Corale. "You got a room for me?"

"How's 417 sound, Charlie?"

"You tell me."

"I'll put ya down for a night?"

Rankin nodded. "And give me a call at four-fifteen."

The room's high ceiling was faded yellow suggesting whoever had recently painted off-white three-quarters of the way up

to it hadn't had a ladder high enough to finish the job. Rankin heard coming from behind a door left of him pool balls clacking together; a fried-food smell seemed to have its source in there too. He scrawled his name in the register. The deskman handed him a key, told him the elevator was broke, then nodded to a metal door behind him. "One way up for now, Charlie."

* * *

Scrawled names, curses, dates, stick figures fucking and doing whatnot to each other covered the cement walls enclosing the unheated stairway. The heavy, metallic clang of his footsteps reminded him of prison, where every sound, like every emotion and every slight, was magnified. The door out to the fourth floor hallway lacked a spring; the bang it made shutting still rang in his ears as he entered his room, the fourth one left of the stairs.

He put down his bag, tossed onto the bed his peacoat and watch cap, then went into the bathroom. He removed the toilet's ceramic top, reached with one hand into the water beneath it, and felt around until he found a rolled up baggie taped to the underside of the ballcock. He brought out the baggie, unsealed it, and took from it a small scrap of paper wrapped around a key. He unraveled the paper, read the few words on it, folded the key back into it, slid the paper into his wallet, tossed the baggie in the trash, and replaced the toilet cover.

He went back into the main room and unpacked his bag.

He placed his underwear, socks, and sweater neatly in the bureau; hung his two shirts and one extra pair of pants in the closet; put his toiletries in the bathroom medicine cabinet. He took from his front pants pocket his gravity knife and slipped it between the bedspring and mattress. He tried the television, found he could get eight channels on it. He sat down on the edge of the bed, pulled back the window curtain, looked out at the falling white flakes, not one like another he remembered his mother saying. Gaping holes where windows had been made a grotesque smile in the brick side of an abandoned building across from him. John Lee Hooker's voice moaned past the left wall. He pictured time as acres of land under untrod upon snow he'd been dropped in the middle of. He flopped down on his back on the mattress. He put his hands behind his head, studied on a phalange of cracks in the center of the plaster ceiling. He closed his eyes. He saw in his head the impressions left by the cracks.

* * *

In the growing darkness nothing appeared concrete. He saw only abstractions in the room's shadows; in the snow swirling like frenzied piranha amid the greasy light coming from the street side of the adjacent building; in the remnants of a dream in which he'd been in some way churning and rolling—down a hill? in a woman's arms? in the grip of a current? He wasn't sure if he'd been digging or hating the churning and rolling. To stop a harsh ringing in his ears he picked up the phone. "You're a deep sleeper, Charlie."

"What do you want?"

"It's not what I want, Charlie. It's what you want. It's four-fifteen."

The Hooker album that had been playing two hours earlier was still playing. "Okay. Call me a taxi, will ya?"

"Sure, Charlie. Accommodations all right?"

"Yeah, fine."

"Find everything you need?"

This guy's familiarity toward him made Rankin nervous; or that he had information about Rankin did; or the guy in total did. Rankin, instead of answering him, said, "Corale, Ornay, what is that?"

A hesitation on the line. "It's Ornay Corale."

"I'm saying though what sort of name, Ornay, is Corale?"

"Spanish."

"You got to be with a name like that in the White Pages all alone—or close to it—ain't ya?"

"I don't know what you mean, Charlie."

"I mean it wouldn't be like tracking down a guy named Smith or Jones in a small city."

"What wouldn't be?"

"I'm just making conversation, Ornay."

Another silence.

"Hold that taxi for me I don't get down there in time, will ya, Ornay?"

Rankin hung up, not waiting for an answer.

He wiped the sleep from his eyes. He gazed out the window. Now he saw each fracture of dull light as a finger on a hand shaping the greyness, giving it a form as the whirling snow gave it life and the wall of empty windows gave it its hideous face. He got out his knife. Standing up he shoved it beneath his sweater, into his belt. He went into the bathroom, pissed, cleaned his teeth, combed his hair. He came back out and dressed for outside.

He went downstairs to meet his taxi.

* * *

The whirling snow gave the impression of being a single group of suspended flakes. Only a dusting of white powder covered the ground. The temperature hovered at around freezing. Tires hissing over wet pavement; the thump and squeak of windshield wipers; heat blowing loudly through the front vent; crackled voices over the short-wave radio.

He found it odd people emblazoning their names to the world. Ornay Corale.

Edith Icks. Her soft, squishy-looking body brought to his mind cumulus clouds; vats of congealing butter. She had a white lady's Afro; a brown, hairy, quarter-sized mole behind her left ear; a sweet and sour stench suggesting fresh fruit and fish sharing space at an open air market. Determined to tell him things, about the weather, corruption on the local police force, road rage, she didn't care—or took no notice—that he had no interest in hearing them. He said, "Stop at the first shoe store."

"Now you've hit upon an important item." Edith Icks in the rearview mirror nodded knowingly to him. Rankin closed his eyes. She seemed to take his doing so as an indication of his rapt interest in her views on proper footwear. She took off on the value of it to not just the feet, but to the joints, the back, the entire body. Rankin envisioned himself tracking an unidentified quarry through the snow, of following it with the sense of never drawing any closer to it, with a growing suspicion that it, in fact, was pursuing him. He opened his eyes in fear that he was overlooking something, a detail in the here and now that could be his undoing. The cab came to a stop.

Opening his door and stepping out into a blare of voices, horns, engines, he told Edith Icks, "I'll be back in five."

He shouldered his way across the slush-marred sidewalk, through commuters heading home, predators, peddlers, vagrants, shoppers, into a leathery-smelling Payless store that, tucked amid that commotion, suggested to Rankin a snug, underground nest. A beak-nosed clerk in an egg-stained sweater led him at Rankin's insistence to a wall of boots. Rankin elected to try a pair of Gore-Tex-lined Timberlands. He sat down in a vinyl chair facing the clerk, who perched on a knee-high stool. Rankin took off his running shoes to find them soaked through to his feet. "You carry socks?" he asked the clerk.

The clerk already had in his hand a plastic-wrapped wool pair. He unwrapped them and passed them to Rankin.

Rankin got off his wet socks. He tossed them in the trash. He put on the new socks, then the Timberlands. He stood up. The clerk, a yellow-skinned mulatto with a tired breath and a hunched posture, bent forward and felt Rankin's toes. Rankin walked up and down on the rug between the aisles. The clerk watched him. "Plenty of women will let you down 'fore those boots will."

"They act some pinchy."

The clerk again pushed on his toes. He shook his head. "You wouldn't want 'em any bigger."

Rankin nodded. He dropped his running shoes in the boot box. "You got gloves?"

"A whole rack full of 'em up front." The clerk picked up Rankin's sneakers and walked ahead of him to a stand-up display of cold weather hand and head gear next to the cash register.

Rankin selected and gave to the clerk a pair of tan, fleece-insulated driving gloves. The clerk nodded approvingly at his choice. Rankin took a black ski mask from the rack and passed it to the clerk. "You must be expecting the real deal," said the clerk.

Rankin, not saying what he was expecting, followed the clerk to the cash register. A beanpole of a woman who'd been filing her nails rung him up. The total was eighty-nine-fifty. Rankin paid the bill out of his last one-hundred-forty dollars. With a doleful smile, the clerk who'd waited on him handed him his purchases, saying, "You're ready for whatever now."

* * *

The usual sorts of people, it appeared to Rankin, were entering and exiting the terminal; in a fenced-in lot left of it several parked buses wetly glistened under fluorescent pole lights fracturing the near-dark; a couple of the buses were loading or unloading; one was pulling onto the street through the open gate; down the steps of another two cops escorted a madly gesticulating, shouting man in a torn T-shirt and shorts, his words registering in the taxi's backseat only as a single, enraged bellow. "Let me out a block down," said Rankin.

As he paid her the discomfiting thought occurred to him that he would remember Edith Icks, that he would remember other apparently insignificant faces and happenings from his stay here more clearly and far longer than he would want to. After she drove off he crossed the street. He walked back up the sidewalk until he was directly across from the terminal, before a bar and grill called The Depot. He went into The Depot, took a table facing the front window, sat his shopping bag in the chair opposite him, and from a washed-out blonde waitress anywhere between twenty-five and forty ordered a grilled cheese sandwich and a Dewar's with a Budweiser back.

He sat watching the station's revolving front door, not for a particular person or occurrence, but for something out of the ordinary; a thing (unless and until it happened he wouldn't know what) he half-hoped to see and half-hoped not to. He took out and counted his money: forty-two dollars and a small jangle in his pocket. He thought of how little forty-two bucks and change would buy. He studied on the mixture of snow and rain now descending; he tried to picture himself sleeping somewhere out in it. "Bad to the Bone" came out of the jukebox. Two urban cowboys in sundowners playing air hockey left of him yipped and yahooed. A viable-looking body of turbid smoke inched across the ceiling. Placing his order down in front of him, the waitress said of the precipitation, "Nastiness."

Rankin watched her hand, each of its fingers including her thumb wearing a brightly colored ring, pour his beer. "I hate the cold," she said.

Rankin picked up his shot; he tasted it with his tongue.

The waitress placed the half-empty Budweiser bottle on the table. "Not that it does me any good to."

Rankin downed the whiskey. The waitress was still at his back, watching him or watching something outside, beyond him. He chased the shot with some beer. He picked up his sandwich. He realized he wasn't hungry or he was but not for what he was holding. He put down the sandwich and looked up at the waitress. "You got a phone?"

"You mean do I personally"—she smiled at him in a way that might have meant anything—"or do we?"

"Does this place have one?"

She chin-pointed to the far end of the bar. "Between the little girls' room and the little boys' room."

Pushing back his chair, Rankin stood up.

"You're welcome."

"I'll have another Dewar's," said Rankin, heading toward where the waitress had directed him. At the phone he dialed local information and asked for the listing of Maynard Cass. He wrote down the number, put a quarter in the phone, and dialed the number. A female voice answered, throwing Rankin. "Hello?" the voice said for the second time.

Rankin pulled the phone back from his ear.

"Is anyone there?"

Rankin hung up.

He returned to his table. He drained his second Dewar's and the Budweiser. He pictured William Pettigrew sitting on his bunk, his eyes, those big, doleful eyes, hitting Rankin straight on. A few more people came into the bar, after work types. The waitress started to look pretty good to him, which told him he'd drunk enough. His cheese sandwich sat untouched before him, an orangey blob between soggy bread slices. William Pettigrew owned two houses, one in Florida, one up here, and he couldn't even beat Rankin in a game of checkers. The waitress came by and swooped up his empties. "Had enough?"

Rankin nodded.

The waitress pointed to his food. "Bag it or heave it?"

"Heave it."

The waitress slipped his bill under his beer glass, then picked up his plate. "You want more later of whatever you come back, got it?"

"Sure."

"You live local?"

"No."

"That don't matter either."

He left the bar, went across the street, and joined the thickening stream of humanity flowing into the terminal.

* * *

An urge hit him to—before it was too late, before things had gone too far to stop—cash out on a ticket to anywhere; well, to anywhere warm. The Keys maybe. Or L.A. He studied on the ticker flashing destinations above the counter. He experienced the milling crowd around him as one gigantic, circular-shaped serpent, its head connected to its tail, from all its slithering going noplace. Inaudible shouts, bangs, smells reached him. A palpable greyness infected the air. The cities revolving before him—Miami, Minneapolis, Seattle, Cleveland, Houston—struck him, in his flat broke state, as being at once the same city and exactly where he was.

"The storage lockers?" he asked a lady behind the counter.

"Keep heading like you are." The lady's crackly, high-pitched voice, her lips never moving, came at him out of a little gizmo in the center of her throat; it was as if another person lived inside her. Rankin thought of those dolls from which came directionless words in response to being squeezed.

"How far?"

"Take your first Louie," answered a voice at his feet. He looked down and saw a one-armed legless man on a plywood plank with wheels.

"Thanks."

The guy nodded to a jar pinched between his stubs. "Got a buck?"

Rankin got out a dollar and dropped it in the jar, which looked to be fatter with them than was Rankin's wallet. He resumed walking.

Down the corridor to which he'd been directed, in a widened space also containing vending machines, neatly aligned benches, entrances to a men's can and to a women's can, they filled the left wall, maybe a few hundred of them all told. Around a dozen people in the area stood, sat, filtered about. For what—or who—were they waiting? Or were they just lounging? A tightening in Rankin's belly; moist heat on the back of his neck.

He thought again of William Pettigrew.

The sack-like body; the bird-claw hands; the whitish, loose lips tightening only when William the Buddha sucked on one of his little inhalers; the whispery voice, never rising, showing emotion, betraying the thoughts behind it; how the Buddha pissed-off sounded and looked to Rankin like the Buddha petrified, the Buddha Happy, the Buddha joking, the Buddha whatever; how Rankin had often suspected he'd won all those checker games only because the Buddha had wanted him to.

He sat down, facing the lockers, on a bench between a perspiring black guy reading a racing sheet and a yellow-skinned white lady in earmuffs and a pink sweatsuit that reeked of piss. He thought, this shit under the daisies life—people thick as thieves, scarcely a quiet, unsmelly place to perch, smoke-filled air cloying as a close-up dog's pant—live it you become it and the only way not to live it is to beat it, to rise above it, to take your chance it comes and don't look back. He brought out his wallet and took from it the paper-wrapped key he'd pulled from his room toilet. He got off the paper, re-read what was on it, returned it without the key to his wallet. He replaced his wallet in his right hip pocket. He glanced down at the key in his palm; he twice tossed up the key and caught it. He looked at the rows of lockers. He considered how the anonymous masses most times to him were faceless, nearly invisible, then suddenly one of them, like the sloppy-Joe type in an unbuttoned trench coat and Popeye Doyle Hat leaning on the Coke machine across from him, would jump out and become all he could see.

One of the guy's hands was in his coat pocket; the other held before him a half-folded newspaper he kept glancing at then away from as if instead of reading it he was pretending to. A pervert, thought Rankin, a cop or somebody with an even darker agenda than a pervert or a cop, staking out the men's room or staking out the lockers.

Or maybe just waiting on a bus.

Back here, this far from the terminal, he's waiting on one?

Even if the guy is staking out a locker, Rankin told himself, he ain't staking out number one-oh-two because he'd only know to if he got it from the Buddha and the Buddha's interests were flat against him giving out that information. Unless the Buddha's interests had changed. Or unless Rankin had been misinformed by the Buddha as to the Buddha's actual interests (Rankin recalled how a woman's voice had answered Maynard Cass's phone). Or unless Sloppy Joe-against-the-Coke machine had gotten his information not from the Buddha but from somebody (now he thought of Ornay Corale asking him if he'd found everything he needed) the Buddha had been forced to rely on.

Rankin stood up.

He walked down the corridor, past the line of vending machines. He ducked into an alcove leading to a storage room,

out of Sloppy Joe's sight but from where he could still see the
soda machine and lockers. Heading to or from a small plaza of
shops at the corridor's end farthest from the terminal, people
trickled by him. Rankin eyed them for a certain type. A stringy-
haired guy in Army pants, a tattered plaid blazer, and red high-
tops approached him in a few minutes from the plaza. Rankin
reached out of the alcove and touched the guy's sleeve. "Say,
Capt'n."

The guy stopped and peered in at him. Rankin made him for
half-to-three-quarters blitzed. "How's a fiver sound to ya?"

The guy swayed like he was standing in a brisk wind. "What
I have a do for one?"

Rankin dangled the key out toward him. "Go over them
lockers, open number 102, get out what's in it, and walk this
way with her."

"What'll I be walking with?"

"A red-white gymbag."

"With what inside it?"

"Junk. Personal stuff. Pictures my kids."

"Why'n't you go get her?"

"Fella there at the soda machine's waiting on me to show
so's to hit me with back support papers from my ex."

The Captain's eyes rolled sluggishly at the machine against
which Sloppy Joe, making still to read the newspaper, was one-
handedly lighting a cigarette. The Captain looked back to
Rankin. "Nobody gone shoot me?"

"Nobody gone do nothing to ya."

The Captain appeared doubtful.

Rankin got out his wallet and slipped from it a ten-spot.
"You ain't probably got change, do ya?"

The Captain shook his head.

Rankin folded the bill. "I'll have to give ya this here then."
The Captain reached greedily for the cash; pulling it back,
Rankin pressed the key into the guy's palm. "Ya get the bag

walk right past me like I ain't here. I'll come up behind ya, grab it from you 'fore you make the plaza." He pushed the ten into the soiled blazer's side pocket. "What number'd I say, Capt'n?"

The Captain closed his fingers around the key. "One-oh-two."

"I'm a onetime track star ain't lost a step, Capt'n, understand?"

"I ain't going rabbit on you."

"I know you ain't."

Rankin to get him started lightly shoved the Captain in the back. He thought, better safe than sorry. A black kid in a yellow do-rag came full-throttle through the concession area, past the Captain, pursued by two Hispanic kids in orange do-rags being chased by a white security guard. Rankin watched the four of them roar by him toward the plaza, their respective eyes betraying terror, a want of blood, a who-gives-a-shit look. When he gave his attention back to the wall, the Captain was standing perplexedly before it between two men and a girl putting things into or taking things out of three separate lockers. Exhaling smoke around his mouthed cigarette Sloppy Joe had the hand he'd lit up with back in his coat pocket. Rankin thought, maybe not Sloppy Joe; maybe pizza-face with the sailor's bag between his feet and, in his lap, a folded crossword puzzle Rankin had yet to see him add to; or Amazon woman, if it was in fact a woman, in a cheap, spaghetti mop wig; or Mr. lame-looking, over-the-hill hippie in headphones drumming his fingers on his thighs.

The Captain inserted his key into a locker not even close to one-oh-two. He kept trying to make it work as if he was sure he had the right one. Jesus, thought Rankin. He wondered if the guy couldn't read; was too pickled to; had forgotten the Goddamn number. Finally he glanced at the alcove as if Rankin would yell the number at him. Rankin pulled his head back out of sight. He'd of done better, he thought, getting the thing himself. He peered out again to see the Captain showing his key to the girl, who was standing a little left of him. The girl said something to the Captain, in response to which the Captain, incredibly, handed her the key. The girl closed her locker. She walked, a blonde in a wool turtleneck dress, ahead of the Captain, for the wall's other end. Rankin remembered why he'd long ago determined to rely in his life on as few people besides himself as possible.

The girl stopped on the near-side of the two men, just as the older of them lit out with a box he'd retrieved toward the terminal. A shriek sounded in the woman's can; boom-box music blared from up the hallway. The girl slid the Captain's key into the locker facing her, as Rankin detected movement near the Coke machine. Diverting his eyes to the machine Rankin saw Sloppy Joe's backside, in front of a trail of cigarette smoke, disappearing into the men's room. Feeling pulled in too many directions at once he returned his gaze to the girl; she was tugging a gymbag from the locker she'd now gotten open for the Captain. The Captain reached to take the bag from her; the girl instead of giving it to him handed it to the man on her other side or the man, with or without her consent, grabbed it from her. The man took off half-running for the plaza.

Rankin heard the Captain call out a weak, "Hey!" He's got no clue I'm in the building or he knows I am but not where, realized Rankin in the seconds before the thief reached him. He stuck out his foot; the guy, in mid-trot, tripped over it and went down, still clutching the gymbag. In a millisecond, Rankin was on him, his right arm around the guy's throat, his left one pinning the guy's arms to his sides. The guy had muscle, but knew squat about using it. Rankin dragged him, the guy making whispery squeals through his traumatized windpipe, to the back of the alcove. Rankin glanced at the corridor. Passersby, acting deaf, dumb, and blind, tried hard not to look in at them. "You get one chance"—he eased up on the thief's larynx—"to say how you come by the number."

The guy's voice came out squeaky. "Come by what?"

Rankin grabbed the guy's right arm and pushed it up between his shoulder blades. The guy started to scream; Rankin stifled the scream with his other forearm. "In ten seconds I'm out a here, but you might never be." He gave the guy enough air to whisper with.

"I knew what you wanted to hear, Mister, I'd tell you it. I swear."

"You rip off some bum's bag for what, dirty sneakers?"

"You never know who's got what in 'em."

Rankin pushed the arm higher.

"Don't do that, Jesus"—the guy gasped—"I heard him, okay, the bum? tell the girl it weren't his locker, somebody'd hired him. I figured whoever did had to have something in there worth enough to pay a guy to get it." Rankin spun the thief around; pressing his right hand into the guy's neck, he pushed him up against the back wall. In reality or in his imagination the din behind him increased. Any moment someone would raise an alarm. This pretty-boy—thirty or so, dressed all right, stinking of bargain Brut instead of his own sweat—didn't fit Rankin's profile of a bus station grab-and-run man, but then it was a profile he was putting together standing there. A solid object—a gun, a knife, a wallet maybe—made a bulge inside the guy's jacket. Rankin reached for whatever it was and the guy used his freed-up arm to hurl an amateur's roundhouse at Rankin. Ducking the punch, Rankin brought a knee hard up into the guy's groin, finishing him, as somebody out in the hallway started yelling for a cop. Rankin grabbed the bag and split.

He headed at a fast walk back toward the terminal, seeing, as he passed the lockers, the Captain, holding his head in his hands, slouched on the bench next to the lame-looking hippy. A cop hot-footed by him in the other direction. He saw no sign of the girl. Outside it was dark and the precipitation had changed from sleet to a light drizzle.

* * *

Hawaiian-print shirts and sunglasses for sale at a sidewalk booth coated in ice: a shirtless muscle-head doing one-armed dumbbell curls in a canopied doorway; a guy licking his wet reflection in an optometrist's window; a hunch-backed, grandmotherly type to everyone she encountered melodically screaming "motherfucker."

Toting the bag through the rush-hour crowd, sensing that in taking it he'd passed an invisible line which, like a bird flying in front of a gale, he could only move farther away from. After nearly being mowed down in a crosswalk by a Cadillac convertible with its top down, whose snowsuit-clad driver, next to his snowsuit-clad date, blew a red light, he veered into a McDonald's.

Snot-nosed kids screaming. Slick floors. A greasy stench. Young punks fueling up. Old geezers escaping the weather. Coffee drinkers a million miles gone. He waited behind the front door a couple of minutes to see if anyone would follow him in. No one did. He told himself he was being paranoid; he answered himself that his paranoia to now had kept him alive.

He entered the men's room, joining a guy, wearing Jockey briefs over dancer's tights, examining the inside of a Big Mac with his fingers as he pissed into a urinal. "Yours have meat in it?"

Rankin ignored him.

"Ain't nothing in mine but a little transformer."

"Go show 'em," said Rankin.

"Don't think they don't know." The guy turned to Rankin. He pointed to the roll's contents. "Any more than they ain't listening to us this very second."

Rankin walked past him into a stall. After bolting the door, he lay his Payless bag on the floor and the gymbag on the toilet's plumbing. He unzipped and pulled apart the gymbag, revealing inside it, atop a paper sack, a nickel-plated .38 revolver with a silencer screwed to its barrel. He picked up the gun, confirmed it was loaded and lacked a serial number. He placed it back in the bag, under the sack. He heard the guy wearing his underpants outside of his clothes talking to himself or to Rankin or to somebody the guy thought was listening to him through his hamburger. Rankin opened the sack; from a glance he knew it held, in fifty and one-hundred dollar packets, more money than he'd ever seen in one place. He didn't count it; he no more doubted its amount to the penny than he doubted the course he'd obligated himself to. He felt around beneath the sack until he grasped a letter-sized envelope. He pulled out the envelope and removed from it a black-and-white photograph of a good-looking white guy in a nice suit. The guy looked to be in his mid-thirties, had dark hair, a mustache, a fighter's nose, a rangy, health club build. Rankin flipped over the picture; on its back was a hand-printed address. Rankin envisioned himself pushing one of his black men into the Buddha's back row; he saw the Buddha, as he kinged it, nod in his equivocal way.

The bathroom door opened. He heard at least two people come into the room. He slipped the photograph into his shirt pocket, took from the gymbag and put in his inner coat pocket a packet of fifties, then picked up and shoved the Payless bag into the gymbag. He zipped the gymbag. A wiseassey voice past the partition said, "Let me help you eat that, retard."

He didn't feel safe returning to the terminal to leave the money overnight in another locker as he'd originally planned to do; not with that earlier business and with him unsure of who'd orchestrated it. Nor did he care for the idea of stashing it in his room at the Sinclair. He wasn't even sure, thinking of

Ornay Corale, he favored going back to the Sinclair at all. He decided to keep the cash on him until he could find a secure place for it while accelerating his schedule so that his obligation and this Godforsaken city would be behind him by sunup. Squealing came from the outer room. Harsh laughter. Rankin opened the stall door to see a tattoo-covered skin head holding the guy in the underpants from behind while another hairless dirtbag, this one's lips, nose, and eyebrows pierced by a dozen or so tiny, metal studs, force-fed his Big Mac to the underpants guy, who was crying and trying to keep his mouth closed. Rankin didn't know exactly what about the scene made him so angry, though it had something to do with the helplessness of the Big Mac guy. He tried, as the prison counselors had preached, putting his anger into words but gave up and instead clobbered Spikes in the head with the gym bag, knocking him backward into a stall, then, sidestepping the onrushing Tattoo, grabbed Tattoo by the back of his leather jacket and bullrushed him face first into a sink. He turned and, seeing Spikes struggling up from the stall can, nailed him in the left temple with one of his brand new Timberlands. This time the guy stayed sitting. And Tattoo, gushing blood from the center of his face, remained lying on the floor. Rankin turned to the guy in the underpants, who was cowering against the urinals. He pulled back the door to the hallway, held it open for the guy, and told him, "Go out there make them bastards give you what you ordered."

* * *

A block from the restaurant he hopped an east-bound city bus. He put the gymbag on the floor between his feet. A girl maybe nineteen or twenty on the nearly full bus sat down next to him. She took out an emery board and started filing her nails; each was painted a different color. She had blonde, spiky hair; prettiness marred by what seemed to be a permanently stunned look; a fragile-appearing body in a knee-length, baggy sweater; a fresh, piney scent that made Rankin think of some woods he'd lived a few days in after one of the times he'd run away as a kid.

The bus's heater was broken. Words and exhalations came out in white puffs. Passengers bitched and moaned about their discomfort; some, like Rankin, swiped at the windows next to them to clear them of fog. Beyond the glass a smear of building, street, and vehicle lights gave the impression of moving in a continuous band while the bus stood still. Gangsta rap played too loud somewhere at the rear of the vehicle. Laying on his back, alone in a forest of creatures, gazing up through a tunnel in those trees outside of some town or city whose name he couldn't remember (had maybe never even known) at harsh blue sky, at the winking sun, he'd dreamed of what? Taking root and growing a hard, thorny bark there. "Nice."

He glanced at his seatmate, who, after having given him her opinion of his boots, was chin-pointing down at them. "Gore-Tex-lined."

A statement, not a question, from the girl.

She snapped her gum. "Know what they're saying to me?"

"Must be they're whispering whatever it is."

"They're telling me it loud and clear."

Rankin, feeling a touch jumpy, only kept looking at her.

"They're saying here's nobody's mark, a guy with a head on his shoulders, an eye to the future. Somebody knows to take care a business."

She slid the emery board into her purse.

"A man always on the ready, keeps things just so—socks in one drawer, underwear in another, clothes neat in the closet so he ain't got to waste time finding 'em."

Rankin didn't respond to her with so much as a blink.

"Shit, nailed me, you're thinking, and is this a Goddamn

psychic talking at me or what, but even if I maybe am sometimes—psychic I mean—I got your story from the
Timberlands." She smiled; straight, white teeth; pink, healthy-
looking tongue. "Most of who I know with money to lay out on
footgear like yours before the real winter's here'd have come
away with something less practical—rattlesnake hide cowboy
stompers say—instead of taking the forward looking route you
have and 'fore long they'd be pissing to the world 'bout their
frostbit toes."

"Maybe most of who you know's rock-dumb."

She picked up her feet to show Rankin they were in fancy
snakeskin cowboy boots.

Rankin didn't even smile. "They real rattler?"

"A hundred-twenty bucks of eastern diamondback."

"No lining?"

"No nothing but the snake and my freezing dogs in a pair a
socks."

"I'd save 'em for dancing. Buy me warmer ones for walking."

"Knowing that's the sensible course won't make me follow
it feeling how I do in 'em 'cept for the cold." She pulled from
her sweater pocket a lighter and cigarettes. She fired up a
smoke. "Shitty place to live 'round now, yeah?"

Rankin shrugged.

"You ain't got an opinion on it must mean you don't."

"First I come here's today."

"From where did you?"

"South a ways."

The girl blew smoke up at the ceiling. "You ain't giving away
no secrets, huh?"

"Secrets what you after?"

"Ain't that why anybody talks to strangers?"

"I figure people got all kinds a reasons to."

"Suspicion a that kind goes with them boots."

"I got cause to be suspicious of you?"

"I'll say maybe for fear a flat out no'd turn down the excitement."

"You like it up high?"

"Nobody buys boots like these knowing the cold that's coming don't like it all out." She dragged again on her cigarette. She talked out the smoke. "I'm Florence."

Rankin tilted his head to her.

"Way it works now you say what you want me to call you."

Rankin pointed a finger at his chest. "Sam."

"For Samuel?"

"For Samson."

"Like the strong guy got done in by Delilah?"

"First I heard that."

She laughed. "First you heard what?"

"How he got done in and who by."

"Ain't you read the Bible?"

"A little, but a long time ago."

"You ought to go back to it. I do all the time."

"I keep thinking I will."

"What's that they say the road to hell is paved with?"

"I don't know."

She looked frankly at him. "Better for me I didn't either." She dropped her smoke on the floor. "Mine's the next stop."

"Is that Willimette?"

"Alto. Willimette's five miles up in a whole different neighborhood." She squashed the cigarette under her boot. "You got business in Willimette?"

"Later I do."

"How much later?"

"A ways later."

"How you gonna fill the time till then?"

"Maybe get something to eat. They got any places to in Alto?"

"There's a pretty fair pizza joint right below my place."

"Yeah?"

"Take out's all they got though."

"I ain't gonna eat a pizza standing out in this shit."

"I wouldn't want you to either, Samson."

"I ain't used to being called that."

"I'll call it to you if you'll let me."

"Go ahead if you like the sound of it."

* * *

In the Pizza Palace a spray-painted mural showed red ants chasing or following toward safety a lone black ant through a collapsing tunnel; Rankin had the sensation the scene was screaming something the whole world but him could hear.

"A friend of mine, Wheezy—he ain't around no more"—Florence tilted her head at the art work—"done it for a month a free lunches."

On the arms tossing their pie crust Rankin recognized Aryan Brotherhood prison tattoos. Needle-tracks marred the cashier's forearms; into the bag containing their pie he threw two peppermint breath mints.

Rankin climbed with their order behind Florence up the building's external stairs.

Damp, prettified flakes that vanished upon landing had resumed falling in place of the rain. Glazed over streetlights persevered in the gloom like dozens of sick eyes.

Bright yellow and purple paint sloppily adorned her small quarters. No doors were present but to the hallway and bathroom. Veils of beads obscured the other entrances. A male smell mingling with incense tainted the air. Over the back of a kitchen table chair hung a man's shirt. Florence, getting out plates and wine, said, "My ex—he's been gone a few weeks—left some things."

Rankin thought, with more skillful hands he might have been an artist; at times he intuited, as he suspected artists must do, shadings and colors in the world's concreteness. Other times he didn't have a clue. From the silverware drawer Florence took a plastic bag of hash and papers. She rolled a joint, then got it going. Rankin waved away her offer to share it with him. "I got to keep a clear head."

"Whatever in the world for, Samson?"

"I'll need it in Willimette."

"Your mysterious business."

Improvising now, having abandoned what little plan he'd had, Rankin felt more confident than he had since coming to the city. "Your ex still got a key?"

"If he does he ain't used it so's I'd know."

"No roommates gon' pop in?"

Florence cocked her head at him in the way she had at the ant mural. "Was your coming here my idea, Samson, or yours?"

"I ain't clear on it either."

Florence got up, went into the living room, put on some music. "Celine Dion," she said.

"Funny name."

"You got somebody, Samson?"

"Somebody how?"

"Like how I ain't got nobody, 'cept an ex."

"I had a dog."

Florence did a little slow dance with herself. "It's an ex-dog?"

"Guy I left it with while I was in prison said it got run down by a lumber truck."

"How long was you in for?"

Rankin held up all the fingers but his thumb on his right hand.

Florence, agile as a cat, moved in gradual circles. "You do blow?"

"I just told you 'bout that."

"You need a clear head."

Rankin nodded.

"Was it a big dog?"

"Medium big. It looked a lot border collie, some shepherd."

"Did you treat it good, Samson?"

"Till I left it with who I told ya 'bout I did."

"You think it didn't die how he said?"

"I think I put a good dog in the hands of a son of a bitch."
She moved fluidly back into the kitchen. "Mind if I do some?"

"What?"

"Blow."

Rankin shook his head again. Florence returned to the silverware drawer. Grasping his gymbag, Rankin stood up. "I scare ya off already, Samson?"

"I can't answer 'em quick as you ask 'em."

"How I act I want to make a good impression on a guy I can't get a fix on I start asking him questions."

"Makes a bigger one sometimes saying nothing."

"You ain't got to answer 'em truthful or at all you don't want to."

"I don't want to, I don't."

She dropped a baggie containing so little coke Rankin could barely see it onto the table in front of her. "We could set on the couch watch a movie and not talk at all you want."

"When?"

"Soon's we can agree on one. You want to watch a porno movie?"

"You got one that's any good?"

"I got one starring me, how's that?"

Rankin nodded and started for where he'd been headed in the first place. "Soon's I use the john."

* * *

He locked the door, put down his gymbag, then circled the small, rectangular room, pressing his hands against its vinyl walls. Only a spot over the medicine cabinet buckled as if it concealed a hollow spot; short of ripping off the siding, though, he couldn't figure how to get at the cavity.

He climbed onto the toilet seat. He pushed on the particle board sheets comprising the ceiling. The attic rafters prevented the sheets from elevating.

He eyed the room's lower level.

Out of the baseboard nearest him a duct blew hot air; a larger, rusted vent in the floor right of the shower stall looked to be left from a retired heating system. He got off the toilet and squatted over the dead vent, finding it hinged, rather than firmly secured, to the floor joists; he grabbed and yanked on the grill; it creaked up a few inches, exposing a dark hole. Rankin slipped his hand, then his arm to his shoulder, into the hole. His fingers in the darkness straight down touched nothing. He moved them to the right, catching his palm on a sharp object—a nail probably—extending from a stud; he felt atop and under the stud; around six inches wide, it was toenailed to a rafter. He pulled his hand from the hole.

"You're missing the credits!" Florence's voice sounded above the music past the door.

Rankin stood and twisted on the sink tap. He hollered, "I'm coming fast's I can."

He removed the sack of money from his gymbag. He folded the top half of the three-quarters full sack over onto the bottom half, then wrapped around it, and knotted, two long pieces of dental floss from a roll of it he'd found in the medicine cabinet. Careful to not rip or drop it, he pushed the sack into the duct, placed it on the joist, and wedged it beneath the connecting rafter. He shut the grill, pissed, flushed the toilet, turned off the spigot. He went back out to the living room, where Florence, sitting stiffly on the couch before a TV screen on which a girl in a Catholic school out-fit stood in a small room across from a man in a priest's habit and a woman dressed as a nun, said, "I'm of two minds on this."

Rankin put his gymbag on the floor next to the couch.

"Reason I am, Samson, is I've known people—and I don't know or not if you're another one of 'em—to mix an artist up with their art."

Rankin sat down on the opposite end of the couch from her.

"They get all sorts a ideas regarding the one from the other."

"What sorts a ones do they get?"

Florence pointed at the screen, on which the nun, per the priest's instructions, unbuttoned the school girl's blouse. "Concluding for example that's Florence."

Rankin peered closely at the school girl. "She ain't?"

Florence shook her head.

"Who is she?"

"A girl named LuAnn."

Rankin blinked at the screen. "You coulda fooled me."

"Florence, me"—she tapped her chest—"is the actress. LuAnn's somebody else, get it?"

"It ain't you in the uniform?"

"It is and it ain't."

Popcorn started to pop on the kitchen stove. Rankin crossed his legs. LuAnn stood obediently as the nun removed LuAnn's dress, revealing creamy smooth thighs, then her panties, exposing a tiny V of pubic hair. "I had a cat I loved to death for six years that died."

Rankin glanced at Florence. "Huh?"

"Like how you had a dog."

Rankin stroked the side of his chin. Florence looked some embarrassed—or addled; Rankin wasn't sure which. She said, "Florence is sort of shy really. She likes to hold hands, talk even if it's babble, do a little blow to cut the ice."

The nun slipped one of her hands between LuAnn's legs.

"LuAnn—wide-eyed little LuAnn—comes off at first as all sweet and innocent, but what men, what anybody who tries to love her, finds out later is, well—I'll just say she ain't Florence."

Rankin scratched his head. "I know what acting is. I've seen it before."

LuAnn closed her eyes. She put a hand on each of her small, pointed breasts. Her hips pushed against the nun's fingers.

"Florence always worries after men meet LuAnn, Florence will just—disappear to them."

"Was you wanted to watch it."

"You don't want to watch it?"

Rankin swallowed hard. "I don't mind watching it."

"On one hand I'm proud of my performance, you know?"

"It looks to me like it's going to be pretty good."

LuAnn could be heard panting on the screen. "On the other hand LuAnn is so powerful that after seeing her bigger than life what man would want to get to know Florence, I mean"—Florence tapped her chest again—"the hand holder who had a cat she loved that died."

Rankin said, "I ain't never mixed a movie person up with a real one."

"I think you've got layers, Samson, that's what I think." An erection sprouting through his open tunic, the priest approached LuAnn and the nun. "Layers and layers of yourself. Just like an actor."

Rankin said, "That mean you want or you don't want to watch it?"

Florence, answering indirectly, kicked off her boots. "If I put my feet in your lap will you rub 'em warm?"

"What about the popcorn?"

"The popcorn?"

"It might burn."

Florence stood up. "I'll go get it."

Rankin looked back at the screen. If LuAnn wasn't Florence, he thought, maybe Samson wasn't Rankin. He felt better believing it might be so, even while knowing it couldn't be true.

Holding a bowl of popcorn and two full beer cans Florence returned to the living room. "How you liking it?"

"Okay, so far."

"Are you getting aroused?"

"I'm working at it."

"I could fast forward it you want."

"This is okay."

She put the popcorn and beers on the table before the couch. "Hope you like butter on your popcorn."

"Yeah."

"You got out of prison when?"

"Just yesterday."

"Guess you're feeling like a hooked fish thrown back into a pond."

"I ain't forgot how to swim in it."

"What you should do, Samson, is see how much Timberland'll pay you for doing an ad for 'em saying your first purchase as a free man was a pair their boots. What did you buy 'em out of anyway?"

"The same four hundred bucks I had to my name and gave to the state for safe keeping when I got locked up."

Florence nodded down at his gymbag. "I know you're going big time, Samson. I seen it in your boots."

Rankin, looking hard at her, picked up and drank from his beer. The nun's ecstatic moaning, the priest's commanding LuAnn to lick her harder, the cheap, shitty elevator-music soundtrack. He was relieved anyway that no matter what happened later that night his money was safe, nobody could take it off him.

Sitting down facing him on the couch, Florence put her feet in his lap. She smiled timidly. "You don't mind?"

"Nah."

Returning his eyes to the set, Rankin rubbed her feet. They were cold and small, in how fragile they felt reminding him of two little china dolls. The priest entered LuAnn's bottom. "What was its name?"

Rankin gave his attention back to Florence.

"Your dog that died?"

"Mister Full Boat."

She laughed a laugh as small and fragile as her feet. "Mr. Full Boat like in Mr. Full House?"

"'Cause what a guy in a stud game lost to my kings over sixes, he couldn't pay me but with his dog. Mostly, though, I just called him Mister."

"My cat was named Gold. 'Ccount of her color."

Rankin yawned.

Florence's toes nudged him in the crotch. "You hot yet, Samson?"

"Getting there."

"I ain't in no hurry if you ain't."

Florence's talking or the droning sound track or the food he'd eaten was suddenly making Rankin aware of the tiredness he'd accumulated from not having slept, past those couple of hours at the Sinclair, since his release. Florence's voice bore on: how she'd grown up in foster homes in some hick town in Oklahoma, was only truly herself in the poems she wrote and would, if he wanted, let him read, had not taken in another cat for fear it would die and leave her alone like Gold had, had had three abortions and wished she hadn't of, was determined on some days to do anything to get rich and on other days to give away what few belongings she owned and to work among the sick and unfortunate like Mother Teresa had. Once in a while Rankin would glance at LuAnn fucking, sucking or licking and start to get hot, then Florence would say something again and kill it for him. "You're a man of few words," she said.

Rankin just gazed at her, his eyes blinking in their efforts to stay open.

"You want me to take off my clothes?"

Rankin shook his head.

She took out a cigarette, placed it between her lips, started to light it. "I could give you a blow job."

Rankin reached over, pulled the cigarette from her mouth, and dropped it onto the coffee table. Looking funnily at him she blew out the match she'd intended to light the cigarette with.

"Don't you find Florence attractive, Samson?"

"Sure." He tried smiling at her, but he wasn't sure if he managed to. He felt as if he was metamorphosing into somebody else over whose actions and expressions he had no control. He held his watch up before his face. "I'm leaving in an hour."

Florence resumed yakking as if she hadn't heard him, a blizzard of little girl's words; she wanted eventually to fall in love with a well-mannered man, get married, have a family.

Rankin nodded over and over at her; he felt as if his head were on a string being manipulated by a hand extended from the ceiling. He glanced at LuAnn and saw that every one of her orifices and both her hands were full.

"If we could just connect, the two of us," said Florence, "find that human connection."

Rankin blinked at her.

"If we could just find it, Samson, me and you, I believe we'd really have something because I see us as having big potential together. Do you see it that way, Samson? Our potential together?"

Rankin's head bobbed up and down.

"Do you want to fuck me in the ass?"

"Maybe later."

Finally, she started to wind down. Her voice got low, almost a whisper or Rankin had grown so weary listening to her his hearing had diminished. She looked as tired as he felt. The movie ended. Rankin imagined the click it made stopping after the final credits as the sound of her eyes snapping shut; or of his own closing.

Her snoring was the next sound he was conscious of. Her mouth was wide open. Her head lolling to one side. Her hands were tucked under her right cheek, her fragile, little feet still in his lap. She looked about twelve years old. Rankin lay a comforter over her. He stood up. A minute later, carrying in his gymbag, along with its other contents, a flashlight he found under the kitchen sink, he quietly left the apartment.

* * *

Wetly hissing tires, scattered shouts, planes shrieking while climbing from or dropping toward a nearby airport. The windless air at a fraction below freezing. Large, damp flakes trying gamely to stick. A thin, white smear patchily frosting the ground.

A walleyed midget with caked food in his beard and some kind of imitation dimestore medal on his chest asking for change. A close-to-hairless, three-legged dog licking its balls on a Seven-Eleven's stoop. Sporadic lights dully shining behind imprisoned windows. Lewd whistles, catcalls through a titty bar's cracked doorway. Kids peppering with slush balls a boarded up youth center, just ahead of where he veered onto a less-noisy, side street of brick and clapboard row houses bunched together like barnacles on a single rock, the road to both sides lined with parked vehicles.

Seeking, by avoiding hired transportation, to lessen the number of eyes able to link him to Willimette, as well as his overall visibility in the area, he got from his gymbag and slipped on his gloves. They so warmed his hands he only now realized they'd been chilled. He remembered the Buddha claiming but for stupidity jails would be begging for inmates. The Buddha's definition of smart? Being a combination of a clam and a ghost ("Open up to no one and leave no trace of yourself, get it?"). From William Pettigrew, thought Rankin, inside for another ten years minimum.

He sidled up to a black Grand Am, tried its driver door. No dice. The fair number of pedestrians in the area and its harsh lighting dissuaded him from chancing a forced entry. He had a go at, in succession, a Marquis, a Cougar, a rusted Jetta, a tri-toned Trans Am, a Celica, a dinosaur VW bug, a type of mini-van, all of them locked. His lack of luck increasingly felt to him like a warning that he was angling in polluted waters; the appearance of a cop car convinced him of it. He gave it up, hiked to the end of the street and through a small park centered by a gazebo, into a neighborhood of mostly single family, moderately spaced homes. Driveways containing carports or garages adjoined maybe half of them. A few were internally dark. No one but him seemed to be about.

Only the sure thing, he told himself; otherwise, fuck it, go hop a bus to a mall parking lot.

On the grass bordering the sidewalk, he headed along the road, out of the streetlights' arc, not liking the odds any-where—driveways too close to houses, houses too lit up, fences suggesting they restrained dogs, a couple of times only a gut feeling saying blow by her, Charlie—before the last place on the left; illuminated only by a porch lamp the one-level brick-er lay between another darkened dwelling and an empty field abutting the house's sloped driveway. An original model, silver Mazda 626 was backed up into the driveway, under a carport. Rankin walked up the field, parallel to the drive, and over to the car. The driver door was locked so he got out and flipped open his gravity knife. Guessing from its age and model the car would pop easy he slid the long blade into the crack between the door and glass. Glancing through the window as he probed for the lock mechanism he saw the passenger door was unlocked. Feeling almost disappointed, he put away his knife.

He quietly walked to the car's other side, opened the door, leaned into its interior, unlocked the driver door. He lifted up the floor mats, then pulled down the visors; the Mazda's key fell from above the left visor into his lap. Believing good and bad luck were doled out in equal portions to people over their lifetimes, he was wary of receiving at once too much of the good kind and, at the same time, hopeful he was at the start of a night-long streak of it.

A few seconds later he got in behind the wheel; leaving his door open, he rested one foot on the pavement. The house furnace loudly kicked on. In the yard an overturned tricycle sat in a rotted sandbox. Rankin pictured Mr. Mazda Owner cursing him in the morning as a no good, thieving son of a bitch; he felt bad that the kid whose tricycle it was would have to listen to it, would have to suffer who knew what sort of lame shit from a know-it-all guy who gets pissed off at whoever he can reach after leaving his car unlocked and the keys in it and no light on in the driveway; he saw the poor kid, to get clear of it, riding his tricycle way off somewhere then being given holy hell for that too. Bastard, shit-kicker.

He decided he'd bring the car back before anyone wised up to it being gone, that doing so would be best not just for the kid but for him.

He slipped the key into the ignition, the stick into first, the clutch to the floor. Easing off the emergency brake, he gave a good push with his outside foot before pulling the foot into the car and the door quietly closed; he let the vehicle roll slowly down the drive into the street and turned it to the right. The Mazda rolled about fifty feet to a stop in front of the second darkened house. He started it up, let it idle a few seconds, switched on the headlights and heater, and drove off.

* * *

The windshield wipers' squeak and bump. Viperine headlights venting the blackness. Speed and direction from a touch. A familiar boundless feeling; an edgy exhilaration, like swimming naked in a river.

From the main drag he followed a sign for Willimette, 8 miles, to a boulevard of fast food joints, mini-malls, car dealerships, wondering if other sensations prison had suppressed in him would return to him suddenly, as the bang of driving had, gradually, not at all.

In a car traveling in the lane parallel to his he saw a girl who looked like Florence. Then he realized she didn't either, Florence must already have been on his mind. That entire scene; her saying she was and she wasn't the girl in the movie and him wanting and not wanting to fuck her. The whole mix had been bad; at once watching LuAnn, who'd definitely turned him on, doing those things up there, and listening to Florence going on about her Goddamn dead cat. She even had him doing it, calling them—her, for Chrissake—two different names. And her coming on to him, claiming his boots were talking to her, what was that? The way she'd looked at his gymbag, telling him she knew he was going big time. He shouldn't have left the money there. But it had been that or bring it with him. Only now he'd have to return there; he'd made certain of that; he couldn't get his mind around exactly why he'd made certain of it any more than he could get it around the thing he was headed for.

Suggesting a top a good push would set to spinning, an upside down station wagon sat, empty and unattended, on the median. A helmetless Harley rider roared by him on the shoul-

der. From the Mazda's front wheel wells issued a persistent rat-
tle indicative of shot bearings. A mid-eighties dinosaur, older
probably than Florence or LuAnn or whoever the hell, the car
on the open road sporadically burped and lurched. His recent
imprisonment existed in his consciousness as an interminable-
seeming dream from which he'd woken feeling mostly numb.
He recalled an old lifer warning him he'd get to the same place
trying to cull anything worthwhile from his time inside as he
would attempting to figure out where he'd been before he was
alive and where he'd be when he wasn't. Unable to put his finger on specifics, Rankin strongly suspected the experience had
cost him more than time and freedom.

On the increasingly rural road traffic dwindled. Signs of civilization petered out. People, buildings, highway lights disappeared in succession. To his left and right only darkness; ahead
of him the cone of light guiding him, in its invariableness
reminding him again of prison, there when you went to sleep,
there when you woke up, absent only, as the Buddha liked to
say, in your schemes and dreams.

He turned on the radio, found a sports-talk show. He tried
to get interested in it, to act to himself as if he was just a guy
out for a drive. He couldn't bring it off though. He began
thinking seriously about the upcoming minutes. He wondered
if he should have more of a plan than he did. He recalled an
old Charles Bronson movie in which Bronson played an assassin who prepared of each of his marks intricate profiles containing the mark's every routine, taste, habit; from his observations of one guy he'd determined that at a certain hour every
night the guy sat down in his study to read a particular book in
the course of which, again always at the same time, he would
get up to boil water for tea, information Bronson's character
exploited to blow up the guy's oven in his face. The movie was
all right, but who in the real world lived that way—a life so reg-
ulated you could count on it? Nobody Rankin knew. If he'd

learned one thing it was to count on nothing. That didn't mean be sloppy. Or unprepared. It meant, while being careful, be flexible, which, come to think of it, is how he'd come to stash the money at Florence's, to abandon his clothes and toiletries at the Sinclair, and to be driving a stolen Mazda to Willimette.

Willimette, 2 miles.

Ahead he saw the glow of lights from the town's outskirts. In no time he was on another Boulevard that looked no different from the one he'd left ten minutes earlier. The precipitation had lessened. He turned the windshield wipers too intermittent. He surprised himself with how calm and clear-headed he felt. An odd thought struck him that some lives he'd rather not live, that if he were living them he'd as soon someone put him out of his misery. No particular ones, though, came to mind. He remembered the name of that Bronson movie, "The Mechanic," that it co-starred Jan-Michael Vincent. A few hundred yards ahead of the sign "Willimette, Small City on the Rise," he swung the Mazda into the parking lot of a combined gas station, grocery store, donut shop. In the darkest part of the lot, he parked beneath some trees, near a pay phone. He glanced at his watch. Almost 9:30.

He got out of the car. A palpable smaze thickened the air. A feeling told him that the externalities favored him, that from here on only Charlie Rankin could sink him. He envisioned the Buddha nodding to him in solemn agreement. Leaving exaggerated footprints in the smudging of wet snow he walked to the booth. Someone had ripped off the phonebook. He turned toward the plaza; a smattering of vehicles sat before and next to it. In the lighted Krispy Kreme sign over the donut shop both Rs were out. A guy in an Elmer Fudd hat stood beneath the shop's overhang attempting to hand out to passersby literature of some kind. Pulling his watch cap down to his eyebrows Rankin headed that way. The Elmer Fudd guy offered him a pamphlet on the front of which was a doctored photo of a man with pustules all over him burning alive under the words, "Salvation, Before It's Too Late."

His glimpse of the picture convinced Rankin he'd seen the roasting guy in the flesh. His heartbeat sped up. Sweat broke out on his brow. He pointed to the cover of the pamphlet Elmer Fudd was pushing at him. "Who's it?"

Fudd grinned at him. Rankin perceived the guy was a mute. He shouldered past him into the shop. A counter girl, seventy years if a day old, greeted him cheerily with, "Welcome to Krispy Kreme."

Ignoring her, Rankin glanced around for a phone. He saw one in the far corner and a woman talking on it. Still trying to modulate his breathing, he turned back to the counter girl. Smoke trickled from a tiny cigarette nub in one corner of her upturned mouth. Rankin walked past her into the men's room. He took off his hat, splashed water on his face. The face of a Louisiana redneck, name of Biggins, a presser for a while in the prison laundry, came back to him. As unlikely as it seemed, Biggins, he decided, was the guy shown in flames on Elmer Fudd's pamphlet. He looked in the mirror. Maybe not Biggins, he thought. Why are you spending time on this shit? he silently asked himself.

He put his hat back on. He pulled it even lower onto his brow than it had been. He got out of his wallet the slip of paper he'd written Maynard Cass's phone number on and reentered the main room. The woman who'd been on a call passed him, trailing a stale, perfumy stink, on her way toward a fat guy slopping down a headlight at the counter. Rankin took her place at the phone, which was enclosed in a three-sided metal case dangling a chain-length attached to a local phonebook. He turned his back to the room and dialed Maynard Cass's home. After four rings a man answered. Okay, thought Rankin. He listened to the guy say hello three times, then hung up. He opened and found in the phonebook a four page street map of Willimette. After glancing around to make sure no one was watching him he tore out the map, folded it, slipped it into his peacoat's inner pocket. He left, buying nothing and without looking again at the guy in the Elmer Fudd hat or at his proffered pamphlets.

* * *

Old brick buildings with facelifts, cutesy boutiques of the sort that sold nothing anyone he knew ever bought, antique shops displaying in their windows used junk at jacked up prices, restaurants named after famous people, gussied up lunch joints called delicatessens or eateries or bistros backed a creosoted boardwalk on a river cutting through an historic district.

Back from the water, out his left window, replicas of 19th century gas pole lamps lit a maze of poorly-signed, narrow, cobblestone streets lined with walk-ups and brownstones so close together a postage stamp wouldn't fit between them.

The Buddha, for Chrissake, had said a secluded neighborhood; Rankin had pictured a tree-lined, suburban street.

This shit unnerved him.

He recalled how the mechanic would take days, weeks, casing a layout, how he'd go so far even as to take up residence in a mark's neighborhood, how ahead of blowing up the tea drinker the mechanic had spent hours in the front window of a room he'd rented across the road from the tea drinker's apartment eyeing the tea drinker through binoculars. Okay, but that was bullshit; in real life even a moron wouldn't move in next to and suddenly start showing up around the guy; even a moron understood that the fewer connections he had to the dead guy the better for the moron; for conducting business the way he did the mechanic, decided Rankin—as much as he'd liked the film—had to have been more than a moron; he had to have been an idiot.

Still, he wished he'd gotten here an hour or so earlier when the grid of tangled streets wouldn't have been all but deserted (only a couple of restaurants weren't closed up tight as a clam); when he wouldn't have felt so conspicuous inching through the area, hunting unsuccessfully for Viner Lane, fearing he was sticking out like a sore thumb to the few people who were about or to some local busybody staring out her bedroom window. Finally, he drove several blocks past the section, pulled onto a dark cul-de-sac, and stopped the car next to the empty curb. He switched on the domelight. Once more he got out and spread across the steering wheel the map. By his reading of the fucking thing Viner Lane was exactly where he'd looked for it, between two other streets he'd failed to find. What he couldn't fathom was what the historic section had been doing there. Then he realized he'd transposed north and south; the historic section, for God's sake, was on the other side of the river, actually his side of the river, and Viner Lane, which in fact wasn't a part of the historic section, was across the water, not off of River Run Avenue, as he'd been searching on, but off of River Run Way.

He reminded himself that he was smart, so to quit acting dumb.

He remembered, at least, passing a bridge.

He began retracing his route. He checked the time. Close to ten. Buddha had claimed the guy was an owl, that even an early night to him was in the a.m. Of course Buddha had also said the guy was separated and lived alone, which Rankin had to wonder about after a woman had answered his first call. Her being someone besides a maid or visitor who'd by now left the guy's place was a potential complication Rankin cared not to think about. As he entered a metal drawbridge spanning the river, it occurred to him that maybe the guy who'd picked up the second time wasn't Maynard Cass, but a housesitter or whatnot and that the woman was the housesitter's or whatnot's wife or live-in girlfriend. What had seemed to him crystal clear as he'd hung up the phone at Krispy Kreme suddenly struck him as anything but. The thought hit him that he ought to turn around, go back, and start searching for Charlie Rankin because this wasn't him crossing the water.

Then he was to the far side, passing two bundled up black guys with lines in the drink, sipping from bagged bottles on a concrete abutment. He was tempted to ask them for directions to Viner Lane, figuring anybody juiced enough to be out angling in this shit with a hope of catching something besides pneumonia wouldn't recall anyone or anything they saw while doing it, but he didn't want to chance being wrong and doubted anyway they knew much beyond their names. Between marsh land, dotted with scotch pines, three or four estates overlooked the river to both sides of him. Smaller, ramshackle places filled gaps in the woods bordering the street perpendicular to the water. A few hundred yards brought him to an intersection with River Run Way; ahead of him was a gated community named Pine Crest; to his left a 7-11, a grocery store, a mini-mall; in the other direction, sporadic house lights.

He double-checked the map, then went right.

* * *

Modern houses with big lawns and paved drives, between skeletons of barns and farmhouses, on recycled pastureland; the river, silent and dark, pacing the transitory terrain; a sign for the River Run Country Club pointing, quicker than he'd expected to be here, down Viner Lane; thinking, as he made the exit, stealing one thing was like stealing another: a pair of sneakers, a car, a life; rounding a curve; seeing on the asphalt directly ahead of him a prone body; slamming on the brakes, wondering had he just opened his eyes while not being aware he'd closed them or had he only shifted them briefly from the road; the Mazda screeching to a halt in front of an unmoving German shepherd-sized billygoat.

Darkness seemed to have consumed his surroundings. Suddenly he could see no buildings, no vehicles, no headlights in any direction. He opened the Mazda's driver door.

A foghorn blowing out on the river. In the dank air a warmish current caressing like a finger his face. A memory of the Buddha telling him that, given mortality's highwire act, an unnatural or an unexpected death is impossible. An eerie sensation that the goat as he approached it would jump up and charge him. The brown-and-white body showed no signs of trauma. The animal's eyes were open, aimed at the Mazda. It lay on its left side. Rankin knelt down next to it. He put a hand to its neck.

The body was at once dead and as warm as his own. A shiver went through him. The Buddha saying, "People hate it, Charlie, having to admit we're just another upright animal so we invent laws for ourselves we think will distinguish us," then, as if the two thoughts were connected, "Never, for example, is it said that a monkey swallowed by a python died of unnatural causes or that the python is a murderer."

He dragged the goat by its hind feet to the road's shoulder. He dropped it in the high grass there, then returned to the Mazda which he'd left running with its door open. Driving past the body he thought how the goat wasn't long gone from this world, as short as a few minutes, and how it had looked as healthy as any goat still in the world and he wondered where it had come from and if it had been hit by a vehicle or had just keeled over dead. The whole thing gave him the spooks. In less than a hundred yards, he rounded another bend; instantly lights fractured the darkness, most of them shadily illuminating the outsides of what looked to be good-sized houses set, in leafless woods, well back from and to both sides of the road.

He slowed the Mazda.

At intervals the approximate length of a football field the homes sat at the tops of steep driveways; from what he could see of them the first three buildings faced, oddly enough, away from the road. He looked for numbers on their street-side mailboxes; branches obscured two of the boxes; the third had only a name written on it. On the shoulder ahead of him a sign declared "River Run Clubhouse and Restaurant, .5 of a mile." He surmised from the sign the residences he was seeing the backs of were fronting on a golf course. A car going in the other direction went by him. Then headlights appeared in his rearview mirror. The thought occurred to him that, at this hour, in this highbrow area, a local person spotting an unfamiliar car might take note of its tags; if their suspicions were raised they might even call the police with them. Who knew if maybe one of those neighborhood watch groups wasn't about? Even a rent-a-cop. He considered increasing his speed but worried in doing so he'd draw only more attention to himself. Seeing only an external porch light on at the house a little ahead of him on his side, he put on his left turn signal. Before, he hoped, the lights of the vehicle behind him had drawn close enough to him to delineate to its occupants the particulars of his car, he pulled into the near-darkened house's sloping driveway and started slowly climbing it.

For a panicky moment he feared whoever was on his ass would follow him into the drive; halfway to the residence, though, he saw the vehicle's lights pass by on the road below him. He switched off the Mazda's headlights and carefully backed down the incline; at the drive's bottom, he put his headlights back on; in their beam he saw on a mailbox directly in front of him, #202.

Four houses from his destination.

Adrenaline surged through his brain. His heart beat faster. He thought, what the hell am I doing here? The reality hit him that from this point on he had, really, no plan, only a firm intent, and a sketchy idea of how to carry it out. He corrected himself that he did too have a plan, that it called for him to be flexible, to react to the lay of the thing, to get it done however the situation called for, to not be married to some grand scheme—never mind The Mechanic, the guy was a joke—that maybe sounded all right in theory but in practice could as well turn to shit.

Or had he feared by running through the thing too thoroughly beforehand he'd have dissuaded himself from actually doing it?

Pushing the last thought out of his mind he resumed driving.

In less than a hundred yards he passed a single lane road diverting left off the main drag at where another country club sign aimed at a dull halo of light in the trees; Rankin glimpsed through the woods out his window a lighted parking lot containing a handful of cars before a cluster of white stucco buildings. He pictured a smattering of River Run Country Club fat cats getting blitzed on six dollar shots. His mind's eye showed him a big pot holding all the world's money amid people pushing and shoving to get at it and he thought starting at the back of that mess you need snatch what bills you can from the air or from the hands of the people in front of you because from hell to Christmas you'll never shoulder your way ahead enough to as much as see the pot.

He took to counting houses.

On the left, one; two. He ignored one to his right, figuring on the normal numbering pattern that aligned odd and even digits on opposite sides of a street. A third to his left (he could make out only its drive). A few hundred feet farther on, if he'd tallied right, bingo; he saw no mailbox, just a faintly glowing, two-story shape at the top of a snaking, tree-lined drive; then he was by it. A long sedan, making a diesel engine's tinny knock, passed him going toward the country club. Rankin let out a slow breath, watching the car's taillights disappear. He reminded himself again of how smart he was and to keep counting driveways. The road made a big bend. Sputtering how it was he felt as if the Mazda had a huge sign on it and that if another vehicle came up behind him he'd have to re-think the advisability of getting the thing done tonight. He started eyeing the woods for a turn-off into an empty lot or whatnot. The severity of the curve he was in suggested to him he was following the rim of a big horseshoe back to the highway. The Mazda's lights as he came through the bend fell upon what looked to be a dirt path through the trees left of him.

He immediately downshifted, steered onto the path, and stopped the Mazda; its headlights showed him a rutted, puddle-filled trail, wider than the Mazda, running in an unwavering line fifty or so feet through a thin stand of hardwoods.

He slapped off the headlights.

The sky offered not a shard of light. His surroundings darkened as if he'd closed his eyes. Without knowing more about what lay beyond the hardwoods he didn't dare switch back on his headlights; at where it was, though, the Mazda was a sitting duck to the lights of any passing traffic. Easing out its clutch, he started inching the car forward, thinking to bring it up to where the trees ended, then to get out and have a look around. He'd scarcely begun moving when a vehicle was heard approaching from the direction of the club. Hoping his eyes hadn't deceived him about the straightness of the path Rankin released completely the clutch. The Mazda lurched ahead into the blackness. As it rounded the turn, the nearing vehicle's lights danced in the trees across the road. Rankin pushed his foot down slightly on the accelerator. The car's undercarriage scraped and banged on the ground; its front end dropped down, as if it had plunged into a pothole, and didn't come up;

Rankin stomped hard on the gas, causing the Mazda to shoot forward, out of the hardwoods, a moment before the other vehicle passed by to its rear.

He hit the brakes on the edge of an open field.

To his immediate right loomed the outline of a building he feared was a house; then he was pretty sure it was too small to be. He put the Mazda in park, got from his gymbag Florence's flashlight, and stepped out. Angling the light toward the ground, he switched it on, and walked stealthily at the building. Three large tractor-mowers were parked under a metal awning on the side of the structure facing him; dozens of metal poles attached to numbered flags lay on the ground against it; "Maintenance Personnel Only" was posted in white letters across a padlocked bay door behind the middle tractor. Rankin played the light out into the field. In the ground a few yards from him stood a widely spaced line of wooden stakes. Past the stakes lay a wide fairway, then more trees. Maybe eighty yards to the east, in the woods left of and above the fairway, could be seen the faint glow of a light shining outside the house nearest to him on Viner Lane.

He slowly backed the Mazda behind the building and parked it facing the path, hidden to everything but the fairway. He slipped the .38 into his pants-waist, replaced the watch cap on his head with the ski mask, and rolled up the mask so that, as the watch cap had, it covered everything above his eyes.

Holding the unlit flashlight in his right hand, he headed down the rough bordering the fairway, hoping each of the five places between him and number #210 would be as easy to make out as was the first one.

* * *

Chester Rhimes going to beat him shitless unless he shut up, him then not uttering a word all week, Chester Rhimes, who'd not even been his legal stepfather, then going to pound him piss-less unless he cut the dumb act, Rankin making across his mother's dinner table a mute's hand signals to Chester Rhimes, Chester Rhimes bringing it on with a weightlifter's belt, his mother screaming to Rankin that his stubbornness would kill him, Rankin making though not a peep through it all, never again allowing his mother or Chester Rhimes or whoever would be her next Chester Rhimes the sound of his voice.

Faraway hooing, a tomcat's randy screech, his measured breathing, his crunching footfalls on the half-frozen turf.

Feeling in his wordlessness more powerful than he'd ever felt while inwardly laughing—howling—at Chester Rhimes's intensifying fury, which had ended with Chester Rhimes having to lie on the couch with heart palpitations suffered in his failure to pound a voice, to pound even a living sound beyond a grunt, out of a fourteen-year-old boy.

Concealed creatures all around him silently hunkered down in nests, dens, half-million dollar houses.

Unable to recollect if in that week before he'd left his mother's life for good he'd willed himself to be mute or if he had, in fact, lost the power of speech and if he had lost it why had he and by what mystery had it returned to him.

House number five appeared atop the hill before him as a short, skewed stack of giant boxes burning a dull light.

If, though, he had fucked up the count—here or out on the road—how would he know it before he was inside the wrong building?

The Mechanic wouldn't have had to worry about counting; the mechanic would have had the entire operation figured out ahead of time.

The Mechanic, you mean, who stood around on crowded street corners openly watching his marks through binoculars, snapping their pictures, scribbling for just anybody to see his observations of them into a notepad? The Mechanic who smoked a pipe and drank expensive wine in a world where the only policemen were second-rate actors? Do not mention the asshole mechanic again.

A dog bark up the hill made him realize he'd not thought much about the possibility of a guard dog either. Nor about the likelihood of a burglar alarm. He'd not thought a lot about home security at all because in the back of his mind, he now understood, lurked a picture of himself boldly knocking on the front door of #210. He could see how, even at this hour, that might be the way to go.

He could also see where it might not be the way to go.

Suddenly he had a vision of himself underwater, swimming straight up, blind to everything not immediately ahead of him, toward the hope of air. He stepped directly on a set of fresh footprints crisscrossing his own; not dog footprints, not any four-legged animal's footprints, the tracks, in the icing of wet snow past the fifth house, zigzagged out from the trees into the fairway.

The darkness that consumed them showed nothing to him.

Rankin inclined an ear at the field.

He heard the owl's mournful hooing; a shriek of human laughter; footfalls against the soggy ground, coming at him. The thought of a lone person laughing aloud, yards from him, in that impenetrable blackness spooked him. He quietly made his way to the tree line. He squatted behind a large white oak tree. He put his gravity knife in one hand. He remembered as a kid not giving a rat's ass for Bat Man, Superman, Spider Man. He'd wanted only to be Poof Man; able with a snap of his fingers to become thin air, with a second snap to reappear in a whole different place. The outline of an upright figure moving, thirty of so feet parallel to him, toward the hillside materialized. The smallish figure made an abrupt motion in his direction. Rankin ducked. An object landed loudly in the brush near him. More laughter. A kid, comprehended Rankin, blindly throwing slushballs, laughing at the joy of it. A few seconds later, he heard one of the balls enter the woods farther down. Another peal of laughter. The kid slowly melted into the darkness hiding the hillside, leaving Rankin uncertain he'd seen a figure at all or, anyway, if he had seen one, it had been more than a kid's ghost.

He started walking again, hugging the tree line.

The crack of frozen branches; sighs from the traumatized earth; a fluttering of wings so close by he felt, or imagined he did, the wind they'd disturbed against his face. He thought of the Buddha, having nothing to spend all his dough on but illegal prison perks—gourmet foods, wine, books, a laptop computer, even a Viagra hit and a whore now and then though Buddha and the whores had to go at it standing up in the middle of the night in a laundry room stinking of detergent—and payback for the grudges he'd brought with him from the outside world that, with his health and age, William Pettigrew like as not (even the Buddha made his odds of breathing free air again one in three) had seen the last of. Rankin guessed people were what they were till they died unless ahead of dying they got religion and were reborn in better versions of themselves as he'd heard Hank Congel, after forty years of being a worthless bastard, supposedly had been. Before seeing it he nearly walked into a body of water.

Standing at its edge he couldn't tell how big it was; a fingernail-thin sheen of ice covered the small part of the liquefied body he could see. He started walking parallel to it. In twenty-five or so yards the rough ended, where the fairway began. Though it was pitch dark he felt exposed this far out in the open. Diagonally across the water from him, at the top of the hill, stood the house he'd pegged as #210, shining more lights—two downstairs, one up—than any of the others he'd passed. Fearing eyes were gazing his way out of darkened windows he didn't dare switch on his flashlight. He pictured in the quiet night countless creatures holding their breaths inches from him. The disturbing sensation struck him that he was blindly stumbling at an abyss; or into a behemoth set of open jaws. An obscured view of hell as a monster's foul belly appeared to him.

He heard three distinct splashes.

In his mind three birds, in mid-flight, fell dead in the water.

He collided with the wooden rampway to a narrow bridge. The splashes, he realized, had resulted from clumps of half-frozen snow dropping from the bridge into the water it spanned. He stepped onto the ramp, then onto the bridge; he slipped on its iced-over floor and had to grab the railing so not to go over the edge. He looked down and couldn't see the water for the dark. He looked up and saw the same nothing-ness he'd stared into every night of the last four years and for however many nights before that. He looked behind him and envisioned his boot tracks in the snow going back to the Mazda and from there all the way back to whatever rented, man-stinking mattress in whatever flea-bitten room she'd dropped him on.

Another drawn out, hellish screech from the tom.

He pictured the big son of a bitch with its teeth in a she-cat's neck; hooked into her good; back claws digging in the snow for purchase; daring even the devil to stop him from having his way with her.

Gripping tight the rails he crossed the bridge to another fairway or to the other side of the one he was coming from. He thought given a chance he might have been a good golfer, a good athlete of any kind because he had coordination and could run and climb like a monkey. Though he'd never partic-ipated in a single organized sport, people—a few anyway—said as how he could have excelled in any one he'd tried; on top of which he just knew he could have, same as he knew that when his mind wasn't all cluttered up with weird thoughts, as it had been when he was with that girl Florence, he could do for a woman in a way that she wouldn't feel shortchanged after, in a way that she'd feel even grateful.

He cut back across the fairway to the rough, toward the woods, aware suddenly of the sound of his own breathing; each breath like a rip in a canopy of silence. Buddha had said every living thing had a preordained niche and it wasn't always the one they'd hoped for. A turtle, he'd said, didn't choose to walk around, slower than about any creature on earth, carrying a shell on its back any more than Attila the Hun chose to be a barbarian or John Wilkes Booth chose to be the killer of our greatest president. The Buddha sometimes just talked to talk. A lot of what he said didn't amount to shit if you just listened to the words. But it was more than what he said that swayed you, it was how he said it, how he looked at you when he did, how he touched you on the face or shoulder with those fluttery little fingers, how he made you feel as if you were a diamond the whole world but him had missed and your niche a little jewelry box he was going to make you more comfortable in.

At the edge of the trees he stopped. The pulpy stench of saturated earth, of decaying leaves reached him. He felt fractured all of a sudden, as if he were at once standing there at the base of the darkened embankment and standing to his own rear, watching with detached interest himself standing several feet in front of him. Ice-laden branches creaked, groaned, whined under their burdens. Exhaled from the hillside, a dank mist enveloped him in its ghostly shape. A blurred light marked the house, where it sat in a clearing atop the hill like a slightly tilted hat on an immense head. The thought struck him that this person standing before him was a bad bet at this game, that he was the sort to balk at putting down even an animal; at the same time he was telling himself when that door opens, Charlie, bingo-bango. One's resolve, according to the Buddha, was always in doubt, even to one's self, until the crucial moment, when the tiniest hesitation was like a missed stitch that could cause a whole sweater to unravel. He strode forward. In the woods internal blackness he stopped again.

Not even his feet were visible to him.

To lessen the chances of it being spotted by someone looking out from the house, he placed the splayed fingers of his left hand over the bulb of Florence's flashlight before he turned it on. He directed the beam at the ground in front of him. The muted light revealed a sinkhole, a clogged portion of a drainage ditch running next to the field, half-filled with stagnant water his next step would have plunged him into. A rusted lunch pail, a bra, a drowned or all but drowned fox that must have stumbled into the hole and then couldn't get out of it floated in the water. Rankin, inclining at the motionless animal, recalled Buddha telling him, in answer to why he was in prison, that everything was where it was because in being there it foreclosed its being anywhere else.

Maybe he should have just taken the money and run.

He could still take it and run.

He detected a slight movement from the fox. He placed the bulb end of the light against it. It released a pathetic whimper to his ears.

The half-Cherokee one two ahead of Chester Rhimes, missing two fingers on his left hand—Rankin couldn't even remember his name—calling him a faggot pussy for curling up and sniveling over a few whacks with the flat end of a coal shovel; his mother telling him, why you always gotta get him started, Charlie? You know how he is.

He looked at the sinkhole's partially collapsed banks where the fox had tried to claw its way free.

He abruptly pushed the animal under the water with the flashlight.

The submerged yellow shaft exposed at the hole's mud bottom beer cans, a couple of golf balls. He felt the fox faintly struggling. The knowledge struck him that he was here only because Buddha was convinced beyond a shadow of a doubt that above anyone he could have hired to be here Rankin would not take William Pettigrew's money and run; that he'd do the job. He reached down, grasped the fox by the back of its neck and, suddenly thinking to save it, lifted it out of the hole. He lay it on the bank. He felt duped. The body looked to him now as if it had been dead for days, weeks.

Looking in the mirror—maybe he'd been twelve—and seeing in it no one he'd ever seen before; wondering, with a twinge of remorse for little, sniveling Charlie, if dying meant waking up one day to a stranger's face.

He jumped over the sinkhole.

How, after everything, a part of him—as unbelievable and infuriating as it was to another part of him—longed still to hear that other voice, the one she sometimes talked to him in when it was just the two of them, when there was no son of a bitch coming between them, running her fingers over his face where it lay on the pillow, telling about Humpty Dumpty or Mother Hubbard or, her favorite, Alice in Wonderland.

He played the light to his right.

He followed the shaded beam through the tightly spaced trees, mostly oak and maple according to their downed leaves, along the drainage ditch, until he came to a three-strand barbwire fence. He climbed carefully between the strands, directly onto a path extending from the hilltop toward the golf course. He pictured himself buying with some of Buddha's cash a ride that wouldn't embarrass him to be seen in—a Trans Am or Mustang maybe—tracking her down, and driving up to her place blowing the car's horn, then taking from its backseat and giving to her all sorts of nice gifts, clothes, jewelry, a big screen TV. Then he thought, nah, if she was even alive, if some Chester Rhimes type by now hadn't killed her, he hadn't a clue to finding her and, anyway, he couldn't picture anything after the part where he gave her the gifts.

Saplings, briers, berry bushes filled the spaces between the trees. In the damp shellacking of near-snow his light delineated occasional paw marks and at least one set of larger, indistinct tracks. By morning, he guessed, the night's prints, including his own, would be obliterated by, depending on if the temperature rose or fell, rain or denser snow. Roots, stumps, the tops of buried rocks marred the path. Tripping once, he kept from falling only by catching himself with his extended left hand while releasing a loud grunt. He thought were he someone nearby hearing that ape-like sound in the dark he'd have been the hell up a tree. He smeared with his foot his glove print, then wiped the hand wearing the glove on a branch. He resumed walking. Rounding the next corner he saw the house not thirty yards above him, now showing one light upstairs and one down, overlooking the course to the west. From a corner of a second tier deck a spotlight bathed in soft yellow tones the woods immediately beneath it. Rankin snapped off his light. He stepped off the path. He crouched down facing the structure behind a Juneberry bush. The out of synch thought occurred to him that since getting out of prison he'd not looked around even a little bit to see how the world might've changed in four years.

The house was an octagonal shape.

The second floor's four back sides, fronted by the rounded deck, stood like a ship's crow's nest over the treetops, providing a view of the fields past them. The walls he could see looked to be mostly glass, covered by curtains. In the part of the upstairs farthest from him a small, lighted area glowed orange through its drapes. A larger room toward the center of the lower level was lighted too. A big, circular hot tub sat in the deck's near corner. He could make out a section of metal fence to the building's far right looking as if it might, in its entirety, surround an in-ground swimming pool or—though he hoped not—a dog paddock. He wasn't in for killing a dog. He thought of how for four years he'd gone on believing Mister Full Boat would be waiting for him when he got out and how hollowed out inside he'd felt when a week before his release he'd called Sam Jenkins about picking up Mister from him to find out Mister was dead. "Didn't he tell ya?" said Jenkins's wife, then on came Jenkins with some shit about Mister running out in front of a lumber truck a month or so back and, gee, he'd guessed he'd forgot to write Rankin with it.

That, thought Rankin, was what came from knowing only criminals; he'd had to trust a reprobate with the only life out in the world he'd cared enough for to want to see again. The more he thought on it the more convinced he became that not long after Rankin had gone inside—maybe on the very day he had—son of bitch Sam Jenkins had shot Mister dead for the thirty bucks a month Rankin for forty-eight months thereafter sent him for dog food. Something died in him from that phone call even prison hadn't killed. He'd had no home waiting, no wife, no family, no girlfriend. After hanging up he'd passed by Buddha's cell and given him the thumbs-up.

He looked at his watch. 11:20.

He brought out the .38, checked again to make sure it was loaded. He put it back in his belt, reminded himself, just in case—God forbid—somebody was there with the guy, to use the ski mask. He stood up and, confident he couldn't be seen through the closed curtains, started up the path, which curled around to his left toward the front of the house. He recalled the Mechanic gassing to a Mechanic trainee about the Mechanic's craft, as if murdering someone took a special skill, as if anybody alive couldn't do it and get away with it, as if it didn't count unless it was done in some half-assed, complicated way, as if the mechanic wasn't just a blowhard puffing himself up for the young guy. He came around the corner of the house and stopped.

A dark-green Saab sedan sat at the top of the drive, before one of two bay doors in the base of the house. Rankin wondered if why the car was outside on such a nasty night was because the garage held other vehicles. A backboard and hoop stood on a pole to one side of the pavement. A snow-topped ball lay beneath the hoop. He pictured kids shooting baskets in the drive. His worry that he'd botched the count, that he was at the wrong place, was renewed. The house suddenly looked to him big enough for ten people. No kids, Buddha had promised. That he'd been for sure on. But what if after Buddha had gotten his information the situation had changed? What if the guy had married a lady with kids and the whole slew of them lived here? Or what if a family was visiting him? He should have gotten more poop from Buddha on the set-up. But Buddha himself had seemed short on poop, at least on poop he'd cared to share with Rankin. Then too Rankin hadn't wanted to know much. He still didn't want to know much, not even why Buddha wanted the job done; but, Chrissake, he needed to know he had the right guy.

The Mechanic would have known way ahead of now where the right guy was and wherever that was the Mechanic would be.

The Mechanic could have walked around with a blue flame coming out his ass because the mechanic was Goddamn Charlie Bronson in a Goddamn movie.

He tiptoed to the edge of the blackness. A lamp over an archway to a flagstone patio at the front of the house shed residual light onto the drive past him. He thought the guy himself could be the hoops player; the garage might be filled with junk, a boat, a million things; how people tell other people they're rich is by having homes, maybe even more than one— like the Buddha with places in Florida and up here—ten times bigger than they need. He took a few steps into the dull light. He halted at the entrance to the patio, a sunken area containing wrought-iron furniture and what looked to be statues of animals and little naked people. Lawn grew on both sides of the patio. A row of rhododendron bushes, their wet leaves drooping like hounds' ears, filled the space nearest the house. A shaded downstairs window several feet left of the front door showed the only internal light.

Rankin proceeded down the walk from the drive, into the patio, peering at the house entranceway for something with the guy's name or the building number on it. He saw no sign or marker in the area; no lettering at all on the door.

Now he wasn't sure what to do.

If he buzzed and anybody but the guy answered he wouldn't know if he had the right house; if somebody other than the guy answered and told him the guy lived next door, he could forget going there and getting the job done after being seen here; and if whoever answered told him the guy was inside, to do the guy he'd have to do the person who told him the guy was inside to keep that person from describing him to the cops later. He might have tried jimmying a darkened window, then, if he'd succeeded, gone inside and poked around for evidence of the guy, only he'd bet his life this place had the latest security system.

Instead, he headed for the lighted window, the half-frozen grass crackling beneath his boots, thinking if the shade wasn't all the way drawn he might see something past it that would allow him to make a more informed decision on whether to chance ringing the doorbell. Three-quarters of the way to the window he stepped on an object that let out a high-pitched squeak; the sound instantly gave rise to a rustling noise ahead of him, like that made by a person or similar-sized creature moving through some brush.

A moment after it began the rustling quit.

Rankin stopped breathing.

Lying night after night in the same darkness as her and who-ever—on the floor or couch of some shithouse motel room or efficiency apartment—afraid to sleep for fear of making an unconscious noise that would remind them of his presence or of the world exploding the moment his guard was down.

He squatted, not shifting his gaze from the dark void the rustling had come from. Holding his breath still, he played his fingers blindly over the crystallized lawn until they located a solid, apple-sized, rubber ball. He brought the ball up to his eyes. Small gashes, like teeth marks, in the rubber.

Breathing as only Poof Man could breathe, so noiselessly that even to them (her and whichever son of a bitch of her countless sons of bitches) in that same dark space with him he was dead or not even there.

He squeezed the ball. It squeaked, only more softly, as it had when he'd stepped on it.

More rustling. Then a mewl or whimper.

Cut the whining shit, ya Goddamn baby, or I'll cut it for ya.

He became conscious of the owl's hooing again, each hoo striking him as a message he couldn't decipher; of the thin, nearly transparent, falling spherules, not exactly of snow, rain or sleet, dampening his skin; of a faint shit odor coming from the yard past the lighted window, where he envisioned, in a paddock formed by the fence he'd seen on the property's lower side, a large creature of some kind—a dog probably, though he'd heard of rich people making pets of wild animals, of lions and tigers even. Placing the ball back on the ground, he quietly stood.

Praying to be Poof Man, able to snap his fingers and disappear to the son of a bitch, disappear to her and to them all, to the whole Goddamn world.

He resumed walking, hoping the animal had reacted only to the squeak of the ball it appeared it was used to chewing on and not from having detected Rankin's scent or footfalls. No matter how lightly he tread he couldn't avoid making a slight crunching noise. He took half of the six good-sized steps he figured would get him to the window's near ledge, heard more rustling, so froze again. He pictured the animal, at the edge of its paddock, nervously pacing, sensing his presence even as its eyes staring out through the spaces in the fence failed to penetrate the same blackness blinding Rankin.

He took another step; then another.

A twig or twig-shaped object snapped sharply beneath his foot.

He braced himself for an eruption from the animal. He heard before him only more rustling.

He thought a guard dog—most any dog—should be barking its fool head off. His realization that the animal might not be a dog, but something less prone to raising a ruckus, relieved him until the thought struck him that maybe whatever was out there wasn't in a paddock either, that maybe the creature so quietly allowing him to approach it was as free as were most of the world's predators to go wherever and do whatever the hell.

Imagining whichever son of a bitch and her being unable to see him, staring right through him even while looking point-blank at him, angrily searching for him in the very places in the room he, Poof Man, was watching them from; keeping himself awake until he was certain they were asleep with visions of them stumbling about, lost, blind, petrified, in the same darkness his X-ray vision permitted him to easily move through.

Lions, tigers—any vicious meat-eating pets—he told himself, would be caged (he was quite certain the law even required it); and actual wild animals—bears, say, or panthers—if they even existed in this part of the country—steered mostly clear of civilization. He got out the .38 anyway.

He put it into his right hand.

He was reminded that he'd never fired a .38, that he'd never fired but three pistols of any kind—a .22 target gun he'd owned for awhile, Sam Jenkins's 9 millimeter (he couldn't help wondering if the same weapon had later killed Mister

Full Boat), and a pearl-handled .45 he'd taken from a Dirty Harry loving asshole after the asshole, on the one burglary he'd talked Rankin into joining him on, had pointlessly blown off with it half the door of an unoccupied house, bringing most of the neighborhood and the cops down onto them—that he'd not fired any of the three at a living target, that he'd never fired a gun period—pistol or rifle—into a person.

The .38 wouldn't become his weapon of choice.

It didn't fit his hand as comfortably as he'd heard a weapon ought to. Because of the smallness of the trigger guard and its nearness to the gun's handle, he had to severely contort his index finger to get it behind the trigger; then, to reach the safety at the guard's bottom left corner, he had to completely withdraw his finger from the guard.

Holding the gun ready to shoot in front of him he slowly moved the rest of the way to the window's near edge. From the forward blackness he heard nothing. He wanted to believe the creature had left; his sixth sense warned him that, facing the same uncertainty he was, it was where it had been when he'd first heard it, trying to envision Rankin as Rankin was trying to envision it.

Stained molding divided the large, rectangular pane into several smaller rectangles; a closed Venetian blind covered all but the lowest two or three inches of glass; slipping from the opening, a dull yellow light landed on, in the space where the column of rhododendrons ended, staked rose bushes growing to within a foot of the sill. Careful not to put his head directly in front of the window, Rankin peered at the shrouded glass above the opening.

Inflamed eyes in a fiery-red face met his.

He recoiled.

Pressing his back against the house wall, panting, he recalled the stranger he'd first encountered in a bathroom mirror when he was twelve, who, instead of going away, had kept showing up until Rankin finally had had to accept the stranger was him. The reflection he'd just seen in the semi-lucent glass was, he understood, of him too, with a chapped face, flecked with ice; at the same time it seemed to him to have been of another person he couldn't place. Then he remembered the guy shown roasting on the front of Elmer Fudd's pamphlet, the guy he'd mistaken at first for Biggins.

An overwhelming urge to bolt, not just from that spot, but literally out of his skin, came over him.

Buddha telling him in the whole world the only sin a man could commit was to deny his niche if he'd been blessed enough to be shown it.

Next time, and every time after this, thought Rankin, he'd use a gun more personalized to him than the .38, a weapon that would feel as much a part of his hand as the keloid scar traversing his palm did.

He crouched next to the rose bushes.

More mewling from the blackness, as if whatever was out there might be sick or in pain.

Buddha saying (in what context Rankin couldn't remember, he hardly ever could remember the context of Buddha's words, just that voice and those hands and those eyes assuring Rankin that Rankin was a special somebody, at least in them) that God and the devil were both ventriloquists so telling them apart in the dark was nearly impossible.

He realized now that what he'd taken for mewling might also have been a low-pitched, throaty snarl; or human laughter muffled by a hand.

If it's Jack the Ripper it can't see me no more than I can it, he told himself, and it likely ain't got a loaded .38.

He looked into the house through the unshaded sliver of glass; he wondered how he'd not noticed smoke coming from the chimney; in a high-ceilinged room lined with bookshelves and hanging paintings a fire burned in a big fireplace; in a chair angled at the window a man read a book before the flames.

Clean shaven, a brushcut, gold wirerims on the guy.

For Chrissake, thought Rankin.

In Buddha's photograph Maynard Cass had a thick mustache, black hair pushed straight back from his temples, no glasses at all.

This guy did have the same health club sort of build and looked around the same age as the guy in the picture from what Rankin had been able to make out of the guy in the picture.

Could be him, he allowed, could be Cass, with a shave, a haircut, reading glasses.

Could be not him too.

After several seconds of studying on the guy he pulled back from the window.

He considered getting the photograph out of his shirt pocket and reexamining it under the flashlight but, with his uncertainty of what was in front of him, he was especially wary of showing a light and doubted, anyway, another look at the photograph would tell him if or not it was of the guy before the fire.

In his frustration, he considered too, to get things over with, shooting the guy through the window, hoping he was the right guy.

Then he thought of the hell shooting the wrong guy would cause him and, anyway, that he wasn't some cowboy went around shooting just anybody, that he was hired to shoot only a particular guy, a guy who needed shooting, according to Buddha, which, with the money he'd been paid, was enough to convince Rankin of it.

He peeked again into the house and saw the guy looking up from his book, directly at him. Forgetting in his surprise at being face-to-face with the guy how difficult it was to see anything in the darkness out of a lighted room, Rankin jumped back from the building. On the slick grass he lost his footing and, making a startled yelp, fell hard on his backside into the rose bushes.

A baying, screechy cry suggestive of a rusty gate-hinge closing onto a screaming person's finger sounded directly in front of him.

Trying to stand Rankin pressed his forearm onto a cluster of rose thorns. He yelped again. Rising to his knees, he yelped louder from a shooting pain in his back. Shut up, he told himself.

A persistent banging commenced as if the animal before him was ramming against a stall or fence. Certain its hue and cry, and probably his own thrashing about, was being heard in the house, Rankin, freeing himself of the rose bushes, catapulted away from the window. He sat against the house, his lower back throbbing, watching for the room light to go off or a human shadow to appear in the window. Neither event occurred. He crept back to and returned his eyes to the crack at the shade's bottom.

The guy was gone, his book open and face down on the chair he'd been in.

Lights started coming on in parts of the house behind him. In the opposite direction the animal repeated its God-awful cry. I know what it is doing that, I just can't put my finger on it, thought Rankin, as a lamp blinked on outside of the front entranceway. He leapt to his feet, understanding the whole deal was turning to shit. He heard a door open in the vicinity of the patio. He looked down at his hand and thought, where the fuck's the .38?, because he wasn't holding it anymore.

He plunged an arm into the roses, piercing in several places the exposed flesh between the end of his coat sleeve and glove. He started blindly searching for the gun, the briers raking his wrist. From behind him or in his imagination he heard approaching footsteps. Christ, Jesus. More shit on the way.

And after the son of a bitch had already hurt him bad in the back, hit it just right, he could tell because it throbbed like a bastard. And these fucking prickers. And that Goddamn animal laughing at me getting it. A light beam or nightmare bounced around on the edge of his consciousness.

The hell's the damn .38? I tell ya to hold onto it and you throw it into a fucking bush like how you never listen to a thing I say, never listen to a thing nobody says. He felt the revolver— or something as hard as it—at the same time he became certain the light beam and the footsteps weren't in his mind.

Playing over the grass several yards behind him, on its way forward, a thin, white shaft.

The crunch crunch of the lightholder's walking.

He tried getting hold of the weapon or the thing resembling it, but his hand lost contact with it. The thought struck him that, with no walls to stop him, he could this time flat-out run from the son of a bitch; then the knowledge came to him in a flash, he'd never run from one again.

He dove headfirst into the roses, tearing his cheeks to hell, not crying out though, not uttering a sound; on the other hand, his loud rifling of the thicket deafened him. Each prick of the briers felt to him like a needle stab in a personalized attack. He imagined the bushes working together to keep the gun away from him, moving it around from place to place, everything but him in that blackness a part of the conspiracy.

In the corner of his eye, the white shaft a stealthily nearing predator.

His frantic, close-mouthed breathing, his clawing at the ground, the son of a bitch's clomp clomping on his way toward him. Then he got hold of it.

He at once felt it beneath his hand, saw his hand in a dull beam, and, feeling like a small fish in a clear blue ocean teeming with sharks, heard a familiar voice say, "Get the hell to your feet."

He looked up to see Chester Rhimes, in one hand directing at him a flashlight and in the other wielding a thick, jagged board.

As if he'd been readying to his whole life Rankin rose to his knees, leveled the .38, and fired it.

The shot's dull pop was softer than Rhimes's grunt at absorbing the bullet; the chunk of firewood Rhimes had flung at Rankin as he'd pulled the trigger banged against Rankin's chest, knocking him into the house wall.

Pain surged from Rankin's lower back down his left leg.

Behind him rose another rasping, prolonged cry, the sound striking Rankin as a mocking laugh, giving him the uneasy feeling the hidden animal (he still couldn't recollect its species from its call) could see him somehow.

He struggled back to his knees. He scanned the ground ahead of him. No one was on it. Then Rankin saw a human shape several feet from where Rhimes had been when Rankin had seen him last, staggering toward the patio, behind the wavering light beam. Rankin raised at the shape his gun hand, registering only now that he'd again dropped the .38.

He plunged back into the briers, scarcely aware this time of the prickers ripping at him. Quickly relocating the gun in the branches of a bush, he grabbed it, from his haunches wheeled back toward the retreating light, aimed and threw two shots at it.

The beam gyrated crazily.

Then it vanished.

Not hearing a thud, Rankin guessed the son of bitch hadn't gone down, that, wising up finally, he'd switched off the light after Rankin had put another round in him, and was either moving forward still or, too hurt to walk, standing in the dark.

Rankin pushed himself upright, unable to suppress a moan at the hurt in his lumbar region. Once he was on his feet the pain eased, but not as much as he'd hoped for. He started walking, with a pronounced limp, at where the beam had blinked off fifty-odd feet before the front door; the lamp over the door cast into the patio a dim, yellow arc, through which Chester Rhimes would have to pass to get into the house or driveway.

Rankin stopped walking, becoming aware again of the precipitation (full-blown sleet now) painfully pelting his face, which was smarting too from the rosebushes gauging of it.

He cocked an ear at the lawn.

He heard only the unidentified animal ramming its paddock, the owl—or a different owl—hooing off in the woods, the driving ice hitting the house, his raggedy breathing.

He reached for his flashlight and discovered it was gone; he must have lost it back in the bushes.

He swiped up a handful of slush, padded it into a ball, and, hoping to flush out the son of a bitch, flung it toward where he'd seen the flashlight go out; above the noise of the falling ice, he heard, after the dull thud of the ball landing, no unusual sound or indication of movement.

Likely he's dead, thought Rankin, and I just didn't hear him fall; then the thought struck him that, long before Rankin had shot him, Chester Rhimes had been dead, and Rankin, now pursuing Rhimes's ghost through hell, as dead as him.

With a sudden, panicky feeling, as if he'd stepped off a ledge at the same time the lights had gone out around him, Rankin ripped off a glove and touched five fingers to his face. It felt to him like a pulpy, featureless blob that nonetheless every son of a bitch, dead or alive, in hell or on earth, could see was the corpse of Little Charlie. His fingers reached to the ski mask ending above his eyebrows.

You ought to have had it on before the son of a bitch recognized you.

Well, I'll put it on now, anyway.

He yanked the mask down over his face to the bottom of his neck.

A weird feeling like, hello in there, who might you be?

Also, a near-giddy sensation, while picturing Charlie Rankin as a mummy no one could see nor lay their hands on without their unwrapping him in the process of which Charlie Rankin would turn to dust.

He pulled his glove back on.

We're the same amount blind, he thought, plus, in this sleet, he can't hear my footsteps. Then he thought, if he can't hear mine I can't probably hear his, which could mean he's miles gone or right next to me. He started moving forward again, listening intently. The mysterious animal once more called out. A hee-haw. A donkey's what, realized Rankin. There's a jackass out there. While putting a name to the creature, he had a premonition of something coming at him; then an object exploded against his chest.

He fell backward onto the grass. Instinctively, he began rolling. He made three and a half revolutions, his chest and back killing him, then stopped, face down in the slop, shielding the back of his head with his hands, praying for the son of a bitch to die and Rankin's mother too for bringing him into their lives.

Finally he realized the son of a bitch wasn't swinging at him. No one was swinging at him.

He rolled onto his back, hyperventilating.

He couldn't count the ways he hurt. Anger he pictured as a blue-white flame burned in him. He felt a want to rip out the eyes of anyone who'd seen him cowering that way. He sat up. His clothes were soaked through. For the third time in ten minutes he'd lost the .38. Playing his hands over the ground, he crawled back to where he'd been clobbered. His left hand landed on a long, tubular wood stick he discovered was attached by a few splinters to an iron shovel blade. The son of a bitch had raised up out of the night and busted a shovel across his chest. That he hadn't stayed around to beat Rankin

senseless after stunning him led Rankin to conclude Chester
Rhimes was bad hurt.

He found the gun coincident to hearing a crash toward the
front of the house. He looked that way and saw in the dim arc
cast by the entranceway lamp a human shape tumbling to the
patio floor after apparently colliding with a statue or piece of
furniture.

Grabbing the gun, Rankin leapt halfway to his feet; pain, in
his chest and back and converging between them, sent him
back down to one knee. "Shit," he moaned.

He saw the shape fifty or so yards ahead of him struggling to
stand and thought if he gets behind the locked door of that
house all the sons of bitches win again and Charlie Rankin
loses again. Two-handedly holding the pistol he drew a bead,
through the sleet, on the rising shape. Melted ice and sweat
dribbling from his hairline into his eyes further impaired his
vision. He squeezed the trigger. He heard the muffled shot ric-
ochet off a statue or the patio's flagstone floor and saw the
shape, now nearly upright, pivot briefly at him, then, dragging
one leg, move off in an Egorish crouch for the house. Estimating
that in two to three seconds Rhimes would be gone behind the
hedge of hemlock bushes bordering the sidewalk to the
entranceway, he releveled the gun. He fired, as the jackass made
another bray; at the sound, he lurched, jerking the shot high.
"Goddamn it!" he hollered.

The shape started around the corner of the bushes. Rankin
was about to loose another round at it, when Rhimes ran into
another object on the patio and went down. He rolled out of
sight behind the hedge.

Rankin once more hefted himself up, all the way this time.
He took off on a hobbled run for the patio. Halfway to it, he
reached an angle from which he could see around the bushes,
part way down the walk. Less than five yards from the front
door, Rhimes was up and moving again in his tortured, one-

sided gait. Rankin, with no time to close the gap between them, stopped dead, spread his legs wide to give himself a solid base, raised the revolver, aimed it at the middle of the son of a bitch's back, and fired.

Uttering not a sound Rankin could hear above the sleet Rhimes careered to his right as if he'd been hit down low on that side with a baseball bat. His upper body dipped as if he was on his way over, as if the slug he'd just taken in his hip or buttocks would finally drop him, but he kept stumbling ahead somehow.

From the distance he was at, Rankin, keeping his outstretched hands around the gun and his eye on the weaving shape past it, calculated the .38 sighted a foot and a half to two feet low. He inched the bead up higher on Rhimes's back, to the base of his neck, took in a deep breath, and, letting it out, pulled the trigger again.

Only a metallic click from the revolver.

He tried the weapon a second time. Even before the hammer hit another blank chamber, from counting up his shots he concluded he'd used them all. He reached into his pocket for more bullets, then recalled he had no more bullets. The .38 had come with a full clip and he'd emptied it.

Feeling as if he'd been thrown, blinded, with his limbs broken, into a cage from which he could hear only snarling.

Shoving the .38 into his pants-waist he started running as best he could toward the house, moaning from pain he could no more stop than the moaning.

Rhimes must have heard or sensed him coming.

At the bottom of the steps, he glanced over his shoulder at Rankin. Rankin had drawn close enough to Rhimes to see his face, but he didn't see it; he saw only the distance the son of a bitch had to cross to get inside, the area he had to negotiate before he could lock Rankin outside. An odd, breathy sound from Rhimes, like air being forced with the last bits of ketchup

out of a squeeze bottle. He turned back to the house, grabbed
the banister, started dragging himself up the stairs.

In the entranceway light growing brighter to him as he
neared it, Rankin made out six steps; at their top, a landing five
or so feet wide leading to a big wooden door; twin cannons
with twigs or dead flowers in their barrels left and right of the
door. Blood as if the sleet were mixed with it on the walk.
More blood staining the stairs; he slipped on some of the blood
as he started up the stairs; to keep from falling onto his back
on the walk he latched with one hand onto the banister; he sat
down awkwardly on the edge of a step.

A pain in his lower back as if its nerves were being twisted
with vise grips.

He heard above him Chester Rhimes scrabbling (from the
noise of it on his knees or belly) across the hardwood platform
for the door; a hissing with Rhimes's breathing suggesting one
or both of his lungs were punctured. Feeling as if he were wit-
nessing the scene he was in from somewhere safely away from
it, yet with his mind absolutely in tune to it, Rankin struggled
to pull himself back upright. Glimpsing Chester Rhimes's buttocks and the rear of his raised head (Rhimes was now crawl-
ing), he heard Rhimes scream, "Open up! Help!"

Rankin thought, could be he's yelling to himself to hurry up
get the door open, to the devil in the hope he'll do it for him, to
any soul in hell to do it, or to a particular person, or persons, in
the house to.

Then he was up and Rhimes was at the front door and
Rhimes was opening the door.

In one excruciating motion Rankin thrust himself onto the
landing and, arms outstretched, lunged for Chester Rhimes as
Rhimes, with mostly his hands, flung his body through the
house's open doorway. Rankin got hold of and tugged on a foot
with a sneaker on it. The sneaker came off in his hands. He
threw it aside and seized a piece of pants above the foot. The

foot still in a sneaker kicked Rankin in the face. Rankin started climbing up the leg he was holding. Rhimes, kicking still, screamed as Rankin must have grabbed a place Rhimes had been shot in. Rankin's gloves and coat and, as he shimmied up Chester Rhimes's body, mask got soaked with blood. The piece of them he was gripping ripped free from the rest of Rhimes's pants. He caught and, trying to roll Rhimes over, yanked at a handful of Rhimes's sweatshirt. Rhimes, face down on the floor just inside the doorway, seized up like a sand crab poked with a stick. Rankin punched at the back of Rhimes's head. Rhimes wiggled forward, slipping a ways out from under Rankin, then, three-quarters-of-the-way flipping over, shoved his right index and middle fingers into Rankin's left eye.

Rankin bellowed, clutching at the eye.

Rhimes stabbed the fingers into Rankin's testicles. Rankin's vision went grey. Rhimes snatched at and tried to tear off Rankin's scrotum, getting hold mostly of the crotch of his jeans and a chunk of his thigh. Rankin reached for Rhimes's neck. Letting go of Rankin's leg, Rhimes grabbed Rankin's shoulders and jerked him forward, smashing Rankin's face into Rhimes's forehead.

Rankin speculated he'd passed out and come to cheek-to-jowl atop his own corpse.

Then he realized the warm body under him was slithering and breathing (a raspy, rattling sort of tremor) and that the bang its skull had made colliding with Rankin's face was ringing still in Rankin's ears and that the body was kissing—no, chewing on—Rankin.

Rankin, roaring in pain, reared back his head.

His bloodied nose, still attached to his face, popped free of Rhimes's mouth.

Rankin glimpsed his mother in her nightgown standing halfway down a stairway before him, watching him. "Go back to sleep like you always done!" he yelled toward her, as Chester Rhimes again whipped his head downward.

Ahead of his plummeting face, Rankin thrust his right fore-arm into Rhimes's face.

Rhimes's teeth or jawbone sharply cracked. His lips opened as if to blow a smoke ring or to form a word beginning with an O. Rankin circled around Rhimes's throat his forefingers and thumbs; he squeezed them together; Rhimes made to pull away Rankin's hands; Rhimes's arm muscles trembled like slapped Jell-O molds. Rankin heard in front of him a scuttling noise and glanced up to see his mother approaching them carrying a fireplace poker, her white, flannel nightgown billowing out from her sides, giving her the illusion of flying.

She reached them and swung the poker at, incredibly, Rankin. Rankin inclined his upper body at Rhimes; the poker bounced off his shoulders into Rhimes's mid-section. Rankin's mother raised the implement above her again. Rankin took from Rhimes's neck one of his hands and as the poker came forward caught it in the hand. He raged at his mother, "Don't you take up for him!" He tore from her grasp and threw across the room the poker. His mother watched the poker hit the wall. She turned back to Rankin. She began to shriek.

Rankin let go of Chester Rhimes, who, smelling of shit and no longer moving, had a purple face with vomit and tooth particles at his lips.

His mother wouldn't quit shrieking.

Rankin stood up. His mother, shrieking still, started back-pedaling away from him. Rankin took a step after her. His mother shut up and, her eyes glued to Rankin, backed up faster. She collided with a table against the far wall. She reached blindly behind her and snatched from the table a glass bowl filled with nuts. She flung the bowl at Rankin. Rankin ducked, the bowl going over his head, nuts peppering his face. He kept walking at her. His mother's hand groping on the table to her rear grasped a portable phone. She started to throw the phone at Rankin, then, as if it had suddenly occurred to her to instead make a call with it, took off running toward the stairs, holding and frantically punching numbers into the phone.

Lunging at her, Rankin got a forearm between her feet. She went down in a belly-flop, the phone skittering across the floor. Rankin pursued her on his knees, hissing in response to his reactivated back pain like a wounded animal prodded with a stick. His mother, slithering after the phone, gave off short, rapid pants; her naked front side (the nightgown had come up over her waist) squeaked on the floor's varnished wood. Rankin got a grip on one of her calves. The foot on her opposite leg lashed out at him. Rankin in his free hand snagged the foot like he would a slow pitched ball.

"No, please!" from his mother. "Help me, somebody!"

Compared to Chester Rhimes she weighed hardly anything.

She screamed at him, "Why are you doing this?"

He twisted her legs, flipping her over. She had on no underwear. Her skin was as white as a corpse's skin; the hair in her groin as sparse and faintly colored as vegetation in a desert. Mascara running all over her face. A perfume smell from her privates; all dolled up for one of 'em. Rankin thinking, what to you was I? A mistake, a single live round some asshole john out of hundreds—thousands?—fired into you that came back out of you as a living thing you took to dragging around behind you with the other worthless keepsakes (that bedraggled red-bottom monkey you claimed to have slept with as a kid, the cracked statue of the Virgin Mary given you by a nun who likely as not was passing 'em out by the dozens from a street corner, a coffee-stained book of poems you only rarely flipped through but thought was something special from the no-name poet who wrote it having scribbled his name into it, a few moth-eaten story books missing their covers an old bird with a hand in raising you supposedly read to you the way a couple times maybe a year you'd read them to me) you couldn't bring yourself to dump. All of it beat up, broken, shit. And me just another piece of it. He climbed up her torso, toward her head. One of his mother's knees came up into his groin.

He fell onto her, groaning.

A gush of air rushed from her lungs. She grabbed and yanked at a clump of his hair. Rankin hammered a fist down onto her breastbone. Her hand fell away from his scalp; another exhale exploded out of her, with the gasped words, "Do it, only don't kill me—"

Blind rage at hearing her take him for just one more son of a bitch (only ten times worse in that he was flesh of her flesh) looking to take a hump from her.

He reached up and grasped her by the shoulders. He grappled his way up her, got astride her belly. He seized her throat in both hands. She pushed at his forearms, whispering, "don't hurt me" or maybe, "look at me . . . "

* * *

"Please hang up and dial again."

He opened his eyes at the space directly in front of him from where he'd heard a voice clearly speak.

No one was there.

He spun his eyes in a circle about the room. He saw only the man he'd earlier seen, reading by a fireplace, now laying mauled and dead in the open front doorway. He heard a noise beneath him.

He looked down.

His index fingers and thumbs were in a white-knuckled clench on the throat of a woman he'd never seen before (her face a contorted, hideous mask with blood-streaked, bulging eyes) urinating onto the floor. Her pee, soaking through Rankin's jeans, warmly touched his knees where they rested on both sides of her waist.

Rankin jerked back his hands.

The head beneath him flopped onto its right shoulder.

"If you'd like to make a call," repeated the voice from the space before him, "please hang up and dial again."

The woman released a sound that recalled to Rankin the donkey's hee-hawing, only a fraction as loud.

* * *

He stood up.

Chester Rhimes ordering Little Charlie to describe to his mother the fuck-up for which Little Charlie, with his pants around his ankles, was about to be strapped raw by Chester Rhimes (a fuck-up clear only to Chester Rhimes who wasn't sharing the secret).

He walked to a high-backed sofa against the facing wall; from the floor just left of the sofa he picked up the portable phone.

Little Charlie knowing that to describe the fuck-up wrong would add to his beating as much, if not more, as would his complete silence.

He turned back to the woman, thinking how'd she get into it?

"If you'd like to make a call—"

A normally pretty woman, he guessed, lying before a stranger to her in her own urine, her legs, chest, face, and neck bruised and scratched, every part of her under her torn, disheveled nightgown visible to the world.

"—please hang up and dial again."

He dropped the phone.

With his right boot heel he smashed it, then ground it into the hardwood.

The woman's eyes followed him as dispassionately as buzzards circle over a dying animal.

Rankin snatched from the couch and carried back to her a knitted afghan.

Her expression said whatever he did to her with the afghan was God's will.

He dropped the afghan onto her mid-section. The woman gazed up at him, as if for instructions from him as to what she should do with the afghan. Rankin turned away from her, as ashamed that his voice had suddenly frozen up in him like that time Chester Rhimes couldn't even beat it out of him as he was embarrassed for her nakedness. He wondered if she'd pegged him a retard. Her painful croaking, her bare skin squeaking on the floor behind him.

He faced her again.

She was sitting up, the afghan wrapped around her. Rankin could see the clear impression of fingerprints on her neck.

An internal voice told him someone needs to finish her.

Buddha saying compassion paved the road to the gas chamber.

"There's money," the woman said in a crepitating whisper. She gazed vacantly at the guy in the doorway. "In his study safe." Rankin wondered what to her the guy was. The woman touched the outside of her throat as if every word coming through it tortured her. "I can get it for you."

Rankin determined to shut the front door so someone going by on the road and gazing up through the trees wouldn't see a shaft extruding from the house. He tried to tell the woman, "Stay put." Only gibberish and spastic movements of his lips came of it. To get across the warning in another way he pointed emphatically at her. The woman shied away from him as if he would smack her. Rankin moved his hands pacifically in the space between them. Again he pointed at her. She only cowered more. His frustration heading toward anger Rankin decided, fuck it. He left her there and strode the thirty-odd feet to the entranceway.

He grabbed the guy by the shoulders, dragged him clear of the door, dropped him, then shut and bolted the door. He'd seen in his head countless dead people (including several versions of his own corpse); he'd seen in reality scarcely any. This one let out noises—an airy fart, an exhale—like a live person. Rankin had no doubt it was dead. With its wide open eyes, paralyzed expression, mangled torso, and shit smell it fit with the cadavers he'd seen in his head. Rankin had trouble believing it had ever been a real person at all.

From a switch near the door he killed the exterior lights.

He returned to the woman, who, since she'd come back from the dead (that's how he saw it) struck him as being too real, even appearing as she did glued to the spot he'd left her in. He motioned to her to stand. Holding in one hand the afghan together at just beneath her neck, she tried with the aid of the other one to rise. She made it only to her knees. She added to the effort with her second hand; the afghan fell off her. Rankin reached down, picked up the afghan; he shielded her body from him with the afghan until she got to her feet; then he handed it back to her. He could see from her face she was hurting. "I'll take you to the money," she said in her haunted whisper.

Rankin shook his head.

The woman gazed numbly at him. Her eyes brought to his mind shot animals staring out from back deep in their dens at who'd shot them. "What then?"

Rankin wasn't sure what. He assessed himself as too lame to retrace his steps to the Mazda and too bloodied to be out in public. He'd have to clean himself up. And do something with the woman. What he would do with her and how he'd come to needing to do something with her he couldn't make himself think about; his mind refused to move past his most immediate need. As if soaping himself he rubbed together his hands, then slid them slowly over his chest, shoulders, arms to convey to the woman his want of a shower.

Giving his gestures a darker meaning the woman said, "I don't—I'm having my period."

Anger the woman must have sensed or seen in his eyes hit Rankin.

She backed up a step. She whispered hoarsely, "Okay." Her eyes moved, as if pulled by a force outside her, to the dead guy. They came back slowly to Rankin. "Just, please, don't hurt me more."

Rankin pictured himself as a photograph of a deformed creature, which at any moment might come to life, the woman was attempting to identify. With the sensation they were taking hours to do so, he watched two strands of her long, blonde hair fall away from her forehead. Thinking to mimic himself shampooing he reached a hand up to his own hair, realizing as he went to run his fingers through it he was still wearing his gloves. And ski mask.

A relieved feeling knowing Charlie Rankin was safely out of sight; knowing he wasn't the mute retard standing before this woman.

He moved briskly his fingers in the air over his scalp.

"I don't understand what you are saying," whispered the woman, her voice bringing to Rankin's mind the sound a wire cleaning rod makes when forced through a rusted gun barrel. "I'm trying to do what you want me to only—"

Rankin seized her by her left elbow, realizing only now how slightly built she was and marveling that her neck hadn't snapped in Little Charlie's hands.

"You don't need to do that," hissed the woman.

In his exasperation at his inability to make clear to her his thoughts, Rankin pulled her with him across the room, past broken chairs, an assortment of nuts, an upturned table, shattered glass, streaks of blood on the floor, into a long, lighted hallway, containing three or four closed doors, thinking one of them had to lead to a bathroom. He stopped before the first one, pushed it open, saw in the hallway light a small space containing exercise equipment and large mirrors on all its walls.

He closed the door. The woman moaned. Rankin eased his grip on her. She whispered, "Maybe you could write on a piece of paper what it is that you're looking for and then show me the paper and I could help you find what's on it."

Rankin wondered if she'd guessed he couldn't write much past his name and was making fun of him for it. He didn't think she looked the sort who would make fun of people less educated than she was but he'd learned long ago that sort looked like anyone else. He pushed her ahead of him to the next closed door. Releasing her arm, he opened the door to an unlighted room; as he stepped past her into the room a voice inside the room said, "Hello, wiseguy."

Rankin darted into the darkness left of him. He yanked out the empty .38.

"Hello, wiseguy." The words came from behind him now.

Rankin spun around in a half-circle, crashing into and knocking down an object taller than him. Struggling to regain his balance he banged into a wall. He heard a fluttering noise and what sounded like a squawk. Then, from in front of him, "Hello, wiseguy."

Rankin with his non-gun hand found and flipped on a wall switch, bathing the room in a soft, yellow glow.

A crow-sized, orange-and-black parrot perched on a floor lamp a few feet before him and its knocked-over cage and above a giant fish tank filled with multi-colored fish, some close to a foot long. Rankin approached the tank. He pushed the .38 back into his belt. He watched transfixed a blue-and-white fish, scarred by what looked to be bite marks, circling the tank ahead of a group of larger, dark-green fish menacingly shadowing it. He remembered a dream he'd started having around the age of ten of killing someone, no one in particular. In each version of the dream he'd kill a person (often a stranger to him) in a different way (with a gun, a knife, a rock, his bare hands, by throwing them off a cliff, by running them down with a car). For a few minutes after waking from the dream he'd feel relaxed, as if he was in charge of his fate. Then he'd get out of bed and see or hear a real person in his world and that safe feeling would disappear.

"Hello, wiseguy."

Rankin looked up at the parrot, looking directly at him. It had small, penetrating eyes that made Rankin feel transparent. Its beak formed what struck him as a disgusted smirk. He thought of the jackass, now this bird and indoor fish the size of lake trout, and wondered what sort of people had he encountered. He remembered the woman. He looked at the doorway.

She wasn't in it.

He ran out into the hallway. It was empty.

He glanced to his left, down the corridor, into the large room he'd trashed. She wasn't there. Jesus! How far could she have gotten, hobbled as she was, in a couple of seconds? Then he realized those Goddamn fish had made him lose track of time; for all he knew they'd hypnotized him into watching them for several minutes while the woman had limped out to the driveway and driven away in the Saab.

He wheeled in a frantic circle, slipping on a wet spot and nearly falling. He looked down to see on the hardwood floor water droplets.

Not water droplets. Piss droplets.

The woman's piss, dripping, he remembered, from her nightgown.

The drops led from the big room up the corridor to, then past, Rankin. Rankin sprinted to the first door on the corridor after the one he'd just come out of. He opened the door onto a dark space rife with detergent. Flipping a switch right of the door, he brought on an overhead light, illuminating a washer, a dryer, a sink, baskets of clothes, mops, pails, cleaning fluids. He withdrew from the room and ran twenty-odd feet to the next door.

It was locked; a sliver of light shone from beneath it.

He pushed on the door. It didn't open.

He rammed it with his shoulder several times. It stayed shut.

He turned his back to the door and mule-kicked it with his right foot, sending a searing pain from his toes into the center of his spine. The door barely budged, even as its lock could be heard snapping. Bracing himself with his hands on the corridor's far wall, Rankin gave the door all he could put into a kick, groaning from the pain it caused him.

The door and something wedged against it from the inside moved inward half a foot.

Rankin put his arms through the space he'd created between the door and wall and, pushing aside a heavy chair behind the door, opened the door all the way into a pink room containing, in the corner nearest him, a baby's crib beneath several ceiling-mounted mobiles, across from a large desk holding a computer at which the woman sat typing next to a telephone off its hook.

That chewed-on blue-and-white fish swimming faster and faster till the sons of bitches chasing it made it so dizzy it couldn't see anything but itself swimming and them right on its ass.

The woman's face and body, from which the blanket had again fallen, so ghostly looking as to suggest that Little Charlie hadn't pulled his hands back from her throat in time, that, sitting there, she was as dead as the guy out front. Her fingers hitting the keyboard, her eyes staring intently at it, as if Rankin, as he strode to and picked up the phone's receiver, weren't even there.

Not so much as a hum came from the receiver.

Rankin wondered if the woman had understood before or after attempting to use it, or if she still didn't understand, that the portable phone she'd taken off its hook in the big room was still occupying the line.

Rankin dropped the receiver onto the desk.

He looked at the monitor; whatever the woman was typing

wasn't coming up on it; the screen displayed only the static message:
Connect Error
The modem has reported no dial tone.

Rankin unplugged the computer. The woman kept hitting the keys. Rankin felt as disgusted at her for typing letters no one could see as he did at Little Charlie for mouthing words no one could hear. He put a hand on her fingers to make her stop. She did, but didn't look up at him.

Rankin hoisted her to her feet. He pulled her over to the crib. He peered into it. But for a neatly made up tiny mattress and a pillow, on which rested a stuffed bear, it was empty. Rankin wondered where the baby was. He hoped it was a long ways from here. He made the woman look into the crib, then at him. She seemed unaware that the afghan no longer concealed her body from him. "There isn't one," she whispered tonelessly.

Rankin, guessing she meant there was no baby, wasn't sure whether to believe her or what to make of what she had said if he did believe her. Her exposed front suddenly reminded him of the parrot's mocking stare at him. He walked to a small, open closet behind the crib and, from among less than half a dozen items hanging in it, took out a terrycloth bathrobe; he handed it to the woman. He half-turned away from her as she mechanically shucked the afghan, put on the robe, slid it off over her legs and dropped on the floor her torn nightgown. She tied the robe. Rankin faced her again. "Please let me help him," she whispered.

Rankin was a moment realizing she was talking about the guy; she didn't know he was dead.

"I won't run from you again, I promise. I'll do whatever you want me to."

A gnawing sensation commenced in Rankin's innards; he pictured a carnivorous animal chewing on them. He wanted desperately to get the hell out of there before whatever it was inside him came out of him through his belly. He walked back across the room to the desk. He tore the telephone's extension cord from the phone and the wall. He returned to the woman holding the cord. "What are you doing?"

He guessed her voice, filled with panic now, had been kindly until Little Charlie had crushed her vocal cords; that she herself was kind; the sort of woman who would, and who would mean it, take up for people like Little Charlie. He forced her to lay on her left side on a love seat next to the crib. "There's no need to—please—I haven't seen your face."

Suddenly the woman, everything about her (her haunted whisper, her piss smell, Little Charlie's handprints on her throat, her blanched complexion, her benumbed look) struck him as being too intensely vivid, as if Rankin had been abruptly thrust into the movie he'd earlier had the sensation of watching her, the guy, and Little Charlie perform in.

He tied her hands together behind her back, then ran the cord down to and knotted it around her ankles. He knew the thing eating him was going to come out of him, he just didn't know when. He shook his head at the woman to tell her the guy was past help and to quit talking about him because it was having a strange effect on Rankin.

He left her there and walked back out into the hallway, then up it to the last door off of it. The door opened into a shiny, tiled bathroom with twin toilets, twin sinks, a Jacuzzi, a steam room, a shower, a full-length mirror into which Rankin peered into the dark, frightening eyes of a masked man caked in blood.

The gnawing in his gut worsening; his mind seeing those handprints on the woman's neck, the bruises on her chest, her standing naked and covered in her own piss over that crib, staring vacantly into it, whispering as if from a thousand miles away, "there isn't one."

He stripped himself of everything but the ski mask.

Charlie Rankin's wiry prison muscles, gained from perform-

ing countless push-ups and sit-ups; the keloid scar running half
the length of his right arm, the result of some son of a bitch (not
even a son of a bitch who'd lived with them, but a twenty-dol-
lar john who'd become enraged at Charlie's mother for not getting from her what he thought he'd paid for and had rushed out
of the room he'd not been getting it in into the room where
Charlie was watching TV) twisting the arm until Charlie's
humerus bone spirally fractured end to end; lash scars on his
back and buttocks, a few left by the half-Indian, most of the rest
by Chester Rhimes, the others by a son of a bitch he'd been too
young to remember past a faceless man inflicting pain; burn
marks on his chest where Chester Rhimes had put out a few of
his cigarettes; a mottled patch of scar tissue on one side of his
neck, evidence of where Chester Rhimes had emptied a bowl of
boiling soup not to his taste; his sprinter's legs, muscular and
tapered, always ready to run; his dick and balls, an accursed
weight between them, growing heavier to him with the years.

The reflected eyes before him refusing to meet his stare, giving the impression of looking through or past him, as if his ski
mask contained only thin air, as if the eyes were engaging
someone standing behind him.

He turned away from them.

His back to the mirror, he removed the mask. He saw in his
mind Little Charlie's face, corpse-white, dead as a shed fingernail. The thing wanting out of him (it felt like a ball growing bigger) moved into the base of his throat. With a herculean effort
he swallowed hard against it, sending it back deep into his gut.

He stepped into the shower and turned it on.

* * *

The blood he washed from his body mostly didn't belong to
him; his only visible wounds turned out to be minor facial and
forearm scratches, on both sides of his nose small gashes

(almost like tooth marks) he had no recollection of receiving, a tender black-and-blue bruise marring his lower back; he directed, in a bent-over posture, a hot jet of water at the spot. The pain radiating from the area lessened. In a few minutes, he found he could nearly touch his toes.

He reminded himself that Charlie Rankin, with all the tight places he'd been in, was still in the deal.

He located in a cabinet beneath one of the sinks a Band-Aid, which he applied to his nose injury. Naked, he proceeded down the hallway to the laundry room; from clean clothes piled in baskets near the dryer, he selected and put on men's briefs, socks, khaki pants, a long-sleeved polo shirt, and a wool sweater (everything fit him as if it had been bought for him). With a duffel bag that had been laying atop the dryer, he returned to the bathroom. He stuffed his soiled clothing in the bag. He put his wallet, knife, and the Mazda's keys in his pants pockets, slid the .38 into his waistband, pulled back on and laced up his boots.

Looking in the mirror to see if he could pass for some golf-club guy, he decided he could as well as anyone could and that if he'd come into the world a little luckier he might have lived in this house, together with the woman in the other room. He tried imagining a life here with her, what they would talk about, etc. "How was your day, dear?", he mouthed, finding himself to be a mute still, and understanding in a flash Charlie Rankin couldn't, in a million lifetimes, have lived here or passed for anyone who did.

He rinsed the blood from the ski mask.

He rung out the mask, picturing again (or else he'd not stopped picturing it since he'd seen it) that blue-and-white, chewed-on fish, and the dark-green ones chasing it; he saw the mangled fish going round and round, with each bite one of the sons of bitches took from it becoming more disfigured and smaller until it disappeared completely, and, then, its specter swimming through eternity away from the memory of those fucking teeth snapping at it.

He yanked the mask onto his head, then down over his face.

A sensation like, uh huh, see ya around.

He reentered the hallway, dropped his bagged clothes near the door behind which he'd left the woman, continued down the corridor, stepped into the room containing the fish tank, and switched on the ceiling light.

"Hello, wiseguy."

The parrot winged past him and out the doorway, as Rankin walked to the tank.

Peering through the aquarium's front pane he counted, by pointing at them, six dark-green fish, each at least as long as his hand, dogging still the blue-and-white one, which he judged to have been further physically diminished since even his last look at it. He seized from a shelf under the tank a small, metal-handled net, plunged it into the water, and scooped up the first fish in the single file line of dark-green fish. He took the fish from the net, lay it on the floor at his feet, then captured and placed aside it the next one in line, and so on, until all six of them were flopping around beneath him. Watching them twisting and gasping for air, he suddenly recalled Chester Rhimes's face as Little Charlie's hands strangled the life out of Rhimes. He looked back into the tank at the blue-and-white fish and saw it still swimming circles, as if it had no idea the sons of bitches had left off chasing it. He felt like crying or pushing over the tank. Instead, he left the dark-green fish dying on the floor and returned to the woman.

* * *

Seeing him in the guy's clothes she widened her eyes at him a second, before, exhaling a distressed, airy sound, she squeezed them shut. Then her eyes reopened and looked at him in the way they'd been looking at him ever since he'd come to and stopped himself from killing her; as if he might be a dead leaf, a blank wall, a curl of dogshit.

A powerful longing hit Rankin that she like him. He thought, if he could let her know him, the real him, who'd never shot a deer or squirrel even. If he could get her to see it had no more been him strangling her than it had been Florence in that movie screwing a priest and a nun. He smiled to her.

Her frightened expression indicated to him she saw him, instead of smiling to her, leering, grinning lasciviously at her. He made the smile less toothy.

She rolled her head away from him.

Rankin comprehended that to her he could be anything, could be less than human, could be a monster, like Frankenstein. To not be afraid of him, she needed to look at him, to see HIM—his curly black hair, his boyish features (angelic, Buddha called them), his cheeks so smooth Buddha said touching them was like touching a baby's cheeks (and if she touched them would she think so too and recognize in him the Charlie Rankin who'd cried as recently as he'd learned of his dog's death?)—because who wouldn't be afraid of a figure in a mask?

He sat down near her head on the loveseat; on the skin to one side of her mouth he placed a thumb, on the other side the index finger of his same hand.

An eerie whistling from her nostrils; her pale lips trembling; her light-blue eyes, flecked with green, angling at him as warily as a kicked-dog's eyes at who'd kicked it.

Little Charlie breaking into an unoccupied house and instead of stealing anything from it methodically taking and crushing under his foot, one piece at a time, every dish, glass, candle holder, and trinket from the home's built-in china cabinet.

He turned the woman's face toward him; with slight pressure from his fingers he caused her to look up at him.

The dark bruises on her neck exaggerating the death mask

color of her skin, her piquant urine odor mixing with her per-
fumed stench, her eyes, in their blankness suggesting shut off
spigots, made him feel as horrible for her as if he were her; he
wanted to comfort her, to comfort himself, as Little Charlie's
mother had sometimes, when no son of a bitch was around,
comforted him. He put his fingers in her hair (Buddha always
telling him his touch was worth more than all his words combined), dirty-blonde hair as silky soft as had been his mother's;
cut to just above the woman's collar line, it brushed pleasantly
his palm as he stroked it. If he could disappear into this sensation, he thought, if he could, anyway, hide in it for a while from
an oppressed feeling that a blunt, heavy object poised over his
head would at any moment be thrust downward, a feeling
going back as far as did his memory.

As he brushed the hair back from them, her ears, in their
delicateness, brought to his mind the sort of handmade choco-
lates sold singularly in sweet-smelling stores he could afford
only to sniff in.

*His mother slipping unclothed into his bed (always when it
was just the two of them) and making him feel for those few tin-
gling seconds safe, making him feel loved.*

"Please stop."

Rankin gazed down at the woman. She looked terrified.
"You don't need to hurt me, I can't—won't—fight you"—her
voice like words from a distant radio station amid a storm.
Rankin, in horror, understood she believed he had in mind to
get on top of her and into her, to make her move beneath him
in the way Little Charlie's mother had taught him to move
beneath her. With the odd sensation he'd been tricked into
gripping and pulling on it as he now was, he released her hair,
then brought his hand up to remove his mask, to show her not
a bad man's face, but Charlie Rankin's face.

"Don't!" hissed the woman, frantically shaking her head, as
if she contemplated him being too deformed to look at. In the

same instant her eyes, for the first time, seemed to Rankin to be trying to find him behind the mask. "I don't think you want to kill me or you would have done it earlier." Rankin could tell talking hurt her; listening to her, he had the impression her words were solid objects being pulled through an opening smaller than them; even while recognizing her pain, he couldn't relate it to anything he, Charlie Rankin sitting over her, had done. "And if you show me what you look like, you might decide you'll have to do it—even if you don't want to—so that I can't identify you later."

Rankin, coming back to his senses (it felt to him almost as if he'd reentered the room after having left it for an indeterminate lapse) understood that he'd nearly made a terrible mistake, that he'd been stopped from making it only by the woman. He had the sensation she'd somehow (maybe through the smile he'd given her) divulged, without seeing him straight on, Charlie Rankin who couldn't kill a deer. From a clock above them a chime rang, signaling 1:00 a.m.; the sound had the effect of returning him entirely to his present circumstances and immediate need to get the hell gone from there.

He pictured Buddha, tapping the side of his balding head, saying, "Think."

Dropping his hand from his face, he abruptly stood up.

Even with his back feeling some better, retracing his steps to the Mazda struck him as a bad idea, if only for the length of the trek and how long it would take him to make it. He extended his hands before him over the woman, and pantomimed steering a car. "You're showing me yourself driving," the woman whispered.

Rankin waved broadly at the wall, to indicate the space beyond it.

"Driving away from here? You're going to leave now?"

Rankin, nodding, stopped waving. He pointed to the woman.

"No, please"—her eyes again looking at him as they had
when he'd had his fingers in her hair, as if she were searching
for the flesh and blood under his mask—"you don't need to
take me with you. I'm no danger to you—I can't hurt you—I
haven't seen you . . . "

Rankin shook his head impatiently at her. Then he made as if
to snatch from her a key, put it into an ignition, and turn the key.

"What?" she said. "You want to leave in a car of mine—
ours—the one in the driveway?"

Rankin nodded.

"You'll go alone"—Rankin felt the woman's eyes seeking
like fingers at the end of outstretched arms to get completely
under his mask, to find him, to touch the flesh of Charlie
Rankin—"I mean, you'll leave me here—like this—if I tell you
where the keys are?"

Rankin only kept staring at her.

"They're on a hook just inside the kitchen doorway," she
whispered hoarsely, "on the other side of the big room, at the
head of the corridor."

Rankin was sorry for her that he didn't dare take time to let
her shower and clean up, that when she was found she'd look
and smell as bad as she did. He eased her restraints to prevent
them from digging into her wrists and ankles and so that she
would be able, he hoped, to eventually free herself. A strong
want to know before he left why it was there, and where was
the baby that belonged in it, led him to look once more in the
crib, then back at the woman; a change seemed to him to have
come over her during the second he'd glanced away from her;
in her face he now saw haughtiness, an assuredness that their
roles had been reversed, that, even tied up, she now held the
upper hand over him. She hissed to him in her tortured voice,
"It's got a full tank of gas."

Rankin suddenly feared those eyes of hers had seen too
much, that she'd recognize him in the future, that, if this was

the last time she saw him, she'd remember forever what she'd learned of Charlie Rankin.

Buddha telling him to be smart, to be a clam, to be a ghost.

Little Charlie thinking that if he shut for good those eyes (Chester Rhimes's and his mother's eyes) they'd never find him again.

* * *

He found himself walking up the corridor, his bag of clothes under his arm; he heard, coming from the room where he'd left them, the dark-green fish still flopping around (the sound fainter than it had been); in the hallway past the kitchen, the fluttering of what he took for the parrot's wings; from his footsteps as he crossed the big room, a creaking that seemed excessive in such a well kept house. Off the floor he picked up and put into his pants pocket a variety of unshelled nuts. Three times, the last while leaving the premises, he stepped over or around the dead guy, not looking at him, not seeing him at all.

The sleet had quit. The air had warmed some. A mist, so thick in places parts of him disappeared to himself in it, had infiltrated the night. For all he heard of the jackass, it might've died in the preceding hours or never existed. He left the Saab behind the storage shed, near where he'd parked the Mazda. At an all night service center on the highway outside of Willimette he dropped into a dumpster the duffel bag holding his bloodied clothes, the ski mask, the .38, and his gloves; he got back into the Mazda, drove it back to where he'd stolen it from, left it as he'd found it, and hiked back to Florence's, where her apartment was yet unlocked and her still asleep before the television that now displayed a solid blue screen.

Intending only to get his money and leave, he felt, standing over Florence, incapable of further activity; at the same time he had the sensation that not all of him was there, as if he was but a small piece of Charlie Rankin, who'd been blown apart and scattered in several directions. He sat down at the end of the couch farthest from Florence's head. He picked up her feet. He put them into his lap. He remembered her pointing down that afternoon, with a fateful smile, at her snakeskin boots over her freezing toes. He commenced rubbing her toes in the way that he'd left off doing hours earlier.

PART TWO

"I guessed you wouldn't be able to stay away," she said at him out of a thin smoke cloud in the livingroom doorway. "That you'd recognized the connection between us, same as me."

Rankin wondered how long she'd been standing there, watching him. He got an uneasy feeling, as if he'd waken to find himself under an X-ray machine. He peeked beneath the blanket over him.

He had on only underpants; a clear salve coated his wrists and forearms.

"Those scratches needed tending to." She dragged down to its filter a cigarette, never touching it with anything but her lips. A female singer's voice oozed softly as a fan's hum from speakers left and right of her. "And it's not hygienic to sleep in the clothes you walk around in."

Rankin, wincing from a tightness in his back, pushed himself into a sitting position. He picked up from between the couch cushions the remote. He flicked on the television. A crater-faced weatherman waved his right arm in a big circle before an aerial map showing clear blue skies.

Walking into the room, Florence said, "You slept through breakfast."

The weatherman sang in a little kid's voice, "Sun, sun, beautiful sun—!"

Florence leaned down at the set and changed the channel; the one she switched to showed a big-haired woman giving live psychic readings over the phone. "And lunch too."

Surprised, without knowing why, his voice was audible, Rankin said, "Eating ought to just be called eating and people free to do it whenever."

"All you ex-cons, I bet, say that."

"Was a rule in there for everything—when to eat, when to shut your eyes, when to open 'em. Without 'em it wouldn't a been so bad."

Florence scrunched out her smoke in an ashtray on the coffee table. "Without 'em it wouldn't a been jail." She touched a finger to his lower back. "This where it hurts you most?"

"Who says anything hurts me?"

"Pain's written all over you."

Rankin backed away from her.

With the first two fingers of her right hand Florence snipped, scissors-like, at the air over his scalp. "You afraid I'll cut off your hair, Samson, make you into a weakling?"

Rankin didn't reply. He tightened the blanket around himself.

"I wasn't, you know, in so many of them porno movies."

Rankin shrugged.

"Seven or eight's all."

"You weren't in none of 'em. That girl LuAnn was in 'em."

Florence nodded. "Been months I mighta starved too without what she got paid for doing 'em."

"I ain't looking for nothing between us past what's happened."

"I didn't climb onto you and fuck you after I stripped you of whoever's clothes you wore back here last night, Samson, which means nothing's happened. I didn't even look at your pecker, though I itched to."

"You don't want to be with me in no kinda way."

"Why don't I?"

"I ain't somebody you'd end up liking."

"You're honest, though. I like that."

"You believe anything comes out a me, you're a damn fool."

"Then I won't believe you're somebody I won't end up liking."

"I don't even like me."

Florence smiled sweetly at him. "But you like me, Samson. You wouldn't have come back if you didn't. Let me rub your back."

Rankin shook his head.

"Let me rub whatever of you hurts most."

Rankin turned off the TV. He suddenly felt more imprisoned than he ever had when he'd been inside, as if everything he could see that would be worth having was locked away from him, as if anything he wanted in the free world (like this girl, Florence) would vanish if he reached for it. He said, "This rich friend of mine in the joint would describe to me all these fancy dishes he loved to eat—things made with lobster, shrimp, veal, grilled swordfish thick as your wrist, only tender and flaky, all these cheese sauces." Rankin's insides suddenly were quivering, as if in the aftermath of a belly punch; he couldn't believe how close to unhinged he felt, as if a tightly wound spool encasing him were unraveling. "One thing to me, I'd tell him, tastes pretty much like another, but he'd say, 'when you get out you go to the best restaurant you can find, you eat the most expensive thing on the menu, you order the waiter around like you're a king, you tell yourself why shouldn't you taste what other people taste, you call me afterwards, you tell me all about it.'"

"You're rich friend write you a check to do all that?"

Rankin stared hard at her. "Don't mention him no more."

"Okay."

"I got money."

Florence, lowering her eyes, made a nervous laugh. "Are you inviting me to a place like that, Samson? Is that what this is?"

"First I'll buy some new clothes. For us both."

Florence gazed back up at him. "And before we leave I'll give you a good bare-naked rub. Take away some your pain, so you'll enjoy yourself on our date."

"I don't want you to rub me. I don't want you to get naked. I don't want either of us to get naked."

Florence said softly, "It might go better between us in that area than you're afraid it will, if you'll let me relax you some."

"Don't you worry about that area. I got no problems in that area."

"I'm not worried about that area, Samson, or any other area. I want us to connect in a big way, is all. I want you to chill. To loose that look from your face that says the devil, in his den, has got a hold of you by one foot and is tugging on it."

"And I'll buy a car."

"A car?"

"After I buy the clothes. And we'll take it to a restaurant where live music is playing and where the help all wear tuxedoes."

* * *

Before the bathroom mirror, he peeled a Band-Aid from his nose; he poured peroxide into a small gash on each of his nostrils; he touched with his right forefinger a circular bruise between his eyebrows.

He put a fresh bandage over the gashes.

He remembered a guy he'd seen on a TV news show who'd woken up on a roadside unable to recall a thing about his life, from which point he'd started a new life. He thought if doctors could do with an operation what had happened to that guy, there'd be no end of people's demand for it.

He brushed his teeth with one of two toothbrushes in a rack over the sink; he shaved with a hand razor he found in the medicine cabinet.

He told himself he'd woken up on this road. Everything before now was down another road. On this road, no sleet, no hail was falling; the sun was shining (he could see it through the slats of the bathroom window) as if yesterday's storm hadn't happened; he was free to go where he wanted, or to go nowhere at all; he was richer than he'd ever been; of everyone she could have been with, this girl, Florence, was with him.

He dug his money out of the heat vent; he put it in his gymbag. He went back out to the livingroom.

* * *

"What did you have in mind to drive?"

"One with guts. And a stick."

Florence, nodding energetically, made as if she were working a shifter in the air space right of her. "The next best thing to fucking back in Oklahoma was closing my eyes and leaning back in the shotgun seat of some farm boy's rip-roarer heading to red-line—Vroom! Vrooom! Vroooom!—'specially coked up or speeding. You want to, Samson, we could use some your money to score with."

"I told you 'bout that."

"You like keeping your head clear. I remember now."

"I'll drink some vodka. Smoke a little weed. That other shit fries me."

"I do better fried. My brain likes me better for heating it up."

"The same friend who said for me to eat at a first class restaurant, told me about this thing—I can't remember what it's called. Them that believe in it think that after they die they'll come 'round again as something else—a rat, a lion, another person even. You hear of it?"

"I wrote a poem about it—'I Remember You from the Treetops.'"

"You figure it happens that way?"

"My poems is the only place I can't lie in. Everything I feel and believe's in 'em. You want to read 'I Remember You from the Treetops'?"

"No."

"I guessed not. If you're not ready to fuck me, you're not ready to read my poems." Florence lit a cigarette. "Do you believe in it?"

"I'd like to."

"If you'd like to, you ought to."

"I'm afraid it's bullshit."

"What if it is? It won't hurt you to believe in it."

"It would if I offed myself to get out of being what I am and into what I'm going to be and found myself in eternal hell."

"That's the saddest thing I ever heard."

"This friend I told you about, he's old and ugly and dried up"—through the smoke surrounding it, Florence's face appeared to Rankin as the sun's image through a cloud—"and whenever I fucked him in the ass he could make himself look as pretty as you."

Florence, cocking her head slightly at him, blew smoke out a side of her mouth.

"He made Charlie Rankin see that he was born to be something, that he could as well be a special thing as to keep being the nothing he was."

"And who's he?"

"What?"

Florence's lips pulling on her cigarette made a snapping noise. "The one your friend said was born to be something. Charlie Rankin."

Rankin envisioned himself imprisoned in fog. He waved at the smoke before him. He remembered Buddha saying the person most dangerous to Charlie Rankin was Charlie Rankin because of the information Charlie Rankin had on the subject. "Just another con—a small timer who acted like he'd been born to be walked on till this friend I told you about—Buddha—give him the right picture of himself."

Florence plucked a shred of tobacco from her lips. "I could fix us up for fifty dollars, Samson."

"What?"

"I'd be back inside an hour."

"Ask me again for toot money and the ride, the meal—from soup to fucking nuts—is off."

Florence laughed uncertainly. "The subject is closed then—Wow! It's not like essential or whatever. It'd a been fun, that's all."

Rankin opened the door to the outside. Florence went up on her tiptoes. She kissed him tenderly on the cheek. "My man," she said, Rankin surprised at how much he cared for the sound of the two words coming out of her, directed at him. They exited into a clear, temperate day (around sixty degrees) lacking any trace of yesterday's precipitation. Florence took his arm. She guided him toward the boulevard mall. "What do you say, Samson, we dress you all in white, and me in black?"

Rankin queried her with his eyes, afraid he was missing in her exactly what he ought to see (what Buddha would call the hay beneath the chaff) while showing her everything in him he was trying to hide.

"All right, then"—with her free hand, Florence smoothed the air before them—"you in black and me in white."

"Why?"

"It'll be fun's why. Jeez, Samson. Ain't we looking to make some noise?"

* * *

He bought himself black jeans, a black denim shirt, a three hundred dollar black leather coat; he bought Florence white wool leggings, a knee-length white pullover sweater, a white beret. He tossed the clothes he'd changed from into a bathroom trash bin; Florence carried her old outfit under her arm in a shopping bag.

They walked up the boulevard's grass median to a used car dealership and bought, for six grand, from a lumpy-faced Indian guy with chili breath and what looked like finger pokes for eyes, nose, and a mouth, a four-speed, fire-red Trans Am, showing seventy thousand miles burned.

"You got a license, Samson?"

"No. You?"

"Uh uh. I've never even drove a car."

"You can drive this one later." Rankin angled the Tranny out onto the boulevard. "Where there ain't as much traffic."

"There's a zoo out this way we could go to."

Rankin strove to reach cruising speed. "What for?"

"To look at the animals."

"To stare and gawk at 'em, you mean."

"I don't think they mind it."

"You can't tell looking at 'em in cages nothing about 'em." In the drabness of prison, he'd forgotten how bright the world could be; reflecting off buildings, vehicles, windows, water, eyeglasses, road signs, the unmasked sun had him flinching and head-bobbing as if at ricocheting bullets. "A deer, say, being the fiercest thing in its paddock, will start strutting around like a lion—it might even believe it is a lion—and a lion, kept fat and happy behind bars, will get to acting like a faggot little house cat."

"Let's go for a picnic then."

"We ain't going to go for a picnic. We're going out to a full-blown dinner."

"I know we are. It's early for dinner, though."

"We've got the scratch they'll serve us anytime. We just show it to them, next you know we're sitting down holding menus. That's how it works at those places."

"Then we should head into the city. All the five star restaurants are in the city."

Wood chips flew out the back of a tractor trailer ahead of them; Rankin had the sensation the blowing particles were trapped in the vitreous body of his eyes, that they were flakes from a large, disintegrating object in his head. He swiped at his eyes, as if to remove the impediments. He said, "I ought to be starved, last I ate."

"You ain't?"

"Goddamn it, I got a right to be"—he jerked the car onto an exit ramp to a one-lane highway—"all the shit I ate the last four years."

"So we'll cruise for a while—take the scenic way in—let our appetites build."

Rankin headed west onto the highway, into open country. He felt that he was, at once, taking in this world he'd recently reentered at half the speed it was meant to be taken in at and with twice the normal power of his senses; but with no feel for scale. He waved at the day past the windshield. "From one to ten, what do you give it?"

"Terms of weather?"

"Terms of whatever."

"Eight, eight-and-a-half. 'Cause you're with me, maybe nine. And I ain't never seen a ten." Florence fished a joint from her purse. "What do you make it?"

Rankin, finding in his memory no day to put this one against and no feeling approximating his current one, shrugged.

Florence pushed in the dash lighter. "This one case worker I had was always telling me, 'you'll feel better when the sun's shining again.' She told me it when I got moved to a group home from the only foster family ever treated me's good as their dog, and she told me it right after she'd told me my daddy had blown out his brains a day after he'd visited me for the first time ever and had promised me he would again real soon." Florence fired up the joint. She drew in some smoke, held it, exhaled it at the roof. "Studies have proved her right too. About the sun."

She passed Rankin the joint. "I seen it on 'Oprah,' some scientist or whatnot saying more suicides, more crimes, more out and out low down and mean things that aren't crimes, happen on stormy or gray days than on sunny ones, that people, overall, feel and act better in the sun."

Rankin hit on the joint, remembering an old lifer name of Bone telling him that everything Bone had done in his youth to get locked up, he'd done when it looked as if the sun would never shine again, that if Bone had seen more sun growing up he might never have served time at all.

Emptying his lungs through the crack at the top of his window, Rankin spotted an AM-PM mini-mart ahead to the right. He put on the Tranny's right blinker. He told Florence, "It ain't doing nothing for me but about blinding me."

* * *

He removed from a sunglasses display in the apparently unoccupied store a pair of mirrored Foster Grants. He gazed into their lenses. Instead of seeing his face, he saw the face of a guy he remembered, at that moment, Little Charlie choking dead in a golf course house the night before.

He placed the glasses on the counter before the register; a cigarette burned in an ashtray over a floor rack of Alto-Willimette Daily Gazettes.

He scanned the front of the top paper in the pile.

No headline about a break-in and murder in the area.

He picked up, then opened the paper.

No mention of a local killing on page two or three.

Nothing about what he was seeing in his mind on page four or five. Or on six, seven, eight, nine. Then he was into the sports. After the sports, were only classifieds. He folded the paper. He dropped it back onto the others.

Behind the register a door marked "Employees Toilet" opened; a bleached blonde with bad teeth, pimply skin, and a six-inch stump for a right arm came out of the room trailing a bad stink. Eyeing Rankin's glasses she pulled from a shelf near her knees and snapped open a switchblade. A radio left of her played a horror movie promo, in which a guy was screaming. Rankin half-recalled another movie character screaming that way; then he realized the person he was remembering hadn't been in a movie—he'd been shot to shit and hollering at his own front door.

"I'll get it off in a minute here," said the clerk.

She was aiming, in her only hand, the knife blade at the plastic price-ring encircling Rankin's glasses. The glasses, with nothing holding them to the counter, kept sliding away from her. The clerk, her useless stump flapping from her side like a busted wing, persisted in poking at them. Rankin reached out and grabbed the glasses; he snatched the knife from the clerk.

He cut off the tag, slipped on the glasses, returned the knife to the clerk, saying, "Nobody'd blame you for robbing the place."

Giving no indication she'd heard him, the woman deliberately folded the knife on her thigh; she replaced it on the shelf; Rankin pictured her as a shell missing its nut, having in it only foul, dead air. He said, "Add to my tab two sixes of Genny Cream. I'll grab 'em on my way out."

The woman rung him up. She told him how much he owed; Rankin picked up she had, with the rest of it, a mother of a lisp. If she didn't mind the world fucking her, he thought, why should he? The thought struck him on the way out that any goings on in that golf course house last night likely would have been discovered too late to make the morning papers.

* * *

"What got you the four years?"

"Taking forty-two bucks and some candy bars from a hospital vending machine I jacked open."

"Sounds like a long stretch for not much."

"I had priors. Plus supposedly I popped pretty good the security guard who caught me at it."

"Supposedly?"

"I don't remember doing it, just being mad at some lip he give me. The state claimed I did and the guard come to court with his jaw wired shut."

Shifting into fourth on the rural highway, Rankin punched the Tranny's accelerator; in the corner of his left eye, a moving patch of fur dove into a thicket.

"Were you wasted?"

"I doubt it."

"You doubt it?"

"I ain't that way often." He switched on the dash radio. He fiddled with the tuner until he found a Willimette station playing hard rock. He looked at his watch. Two minutes to the hour.

"You ever rode in an airplane, Samson?"

"No."

"It's my favorite thing to do."

"How many times you done it?"

"I ain't never done it. I've watched enough of 'em take off and land though to know that when I do do it it'll be the nuts. A few times a year I'll go out to the airport and sit in the terminal, facing the runways, with a nice buzz on. We could do that till you're hungry. You want to?"

Rankin shook his head.

"What's your favorite thing to do?"

"I ain't never thought on it."

"You ought to."

"Why?"

"So you'll know what it is in case you ever do it. And it's a better thing to think about than a lot of things."

Rankin turned up the radio at the start of the hourly news.

"You done a thing like what they said you did and weren't wasted, Samson?"

"I don't think I was."

Florence leaned over and kissed his cheek. "I find that hard to believe, a gentle soul like you."

A DJ reported the top local stories—a burglary at the Alto bowling alleys, an outbreak of hepatitis in patrons of a Chinese restaurant, a proposed raise in county real estate taxes, an upswing in the weather; nothing about a break-in and murder in Willimette.

* * *

"There's a real pretty little church up ahead that's never locked. I know because a guy brought me out here one time on his motorcycle and showed it to me. He said he used to go to it regular until his wife and son died in a car wreck and he stopped believing, but he would still go there once in a while late at night, mostly when he was plowed, and sit in a pew and stare at the stained glass being hit by the moon. It's got real neat stained glass." Florence finished the beer she'd been drinking and carefully replaced the empty can in the carton at her feet. "With the sun being so bright today, I bet it would be something to see."

"You want to see it?"

"I wouldn't mind seeing it. I love churches, even if I don't go to them often."

"I'll take you there and you can see it."

"I want you to see it too."

"I can tell what it is hearing you talk about it."

"That ain't the same."

"Well, it's as close as I'm going to get to seeing it."

"You don't like churches?"

"I don't care one way the other about 'em. I just don't want to go in one."

A horse galloping along the shoulder opposite them carried a woman with the blonde hair and busty build of a woman Rankin suddenly remembered Little Charlie strangling after he'd strangled the guy whose face Rankin had seen instead of his own reflection in the lenses of his sunglasses at the AM-PM Minimart.

Rankin slammed on the brakes.

He jumped out of the car. He stood mid-road, watching horse and rider, until they'd disappeared around a bend a few hundred yards on. He listened to the animal's footsteps fade away. He considered how neither the local newspaper nor the local radio station had reported a double murder or a murder at all last night. The thought struck him that Little Charlie had not killed anyone in Willimette, that Rankin's memories of him doing so weren't but his memories of another one of Little Charlie's bad dreams.

He got back in behind the wheel.

Florence said, "See somebody you know?"

Rankin didn't say if he had.

He put the car in gear. He started driving again.

* * *

Pastures, dotted with cows and horses, between wooded hills, in fading fall color, showing patches of snow at their highest elevations; fields of stubbly cornstalks, mowed timothy, weeds and briars; farm houses, double-wides, a dilapidated trailer park flying a tent-sized American flag; a school looking as isolated and drab as a prison; a creamery, stinking of whey, exuding putrid smoke; a pure white church, a crow plague darkening the sky above it.

"Pull in here," said Florence, waving at a drive leading to the building's rear.

At one end of an empty paved lot hidden behind the church painted lines made a basketball court; the hoop fronted a small grassy area containing a slide, a swing set, a horseshoe pit, around an engraved plaque on a metal pole. A few feet left of the hoop, Rankin shut down the Tranny. "Go see it," he told Florence.

"In a minute," she said, then she inclined at him, put her lips on his, and, opening her mouth, forced her tongue into him.

Rankin pulled his mouth back, but, still locked with his, her mouth followed him; he pushed his tongue against hers as if at a creature invading him; she stuck her tongue deeper into him; her hands fumbled at his belt. Rankin experienced her as a sweet-tasting succubus. She got his fly undone, and a hand on his penis, and started moving the hand up and down. The back of Rankin's head hit the window. He yanked his mouth free of hers.

Little Charlie's harsh pants, with every punch, kick, lash, like the death pants of a small, incapacitated animal being devoured, limb by limb, by a larger animal.

He shoved on Florence's shoulders, propelling her hard into the passenger door.

Little Charlie wondering all the while where his mother was at (in what corner of the room or small apartment she was try-ing to hide, her eyes squeezed shut, her hands over her ears) why she was only ever there for him, loving him in her special way, when no son of a bitch was loving her.

Florence, raggedly breathing, reached down, took her sweater's hem in both hands, and stripped the sweater off over her head, making herself naked, her breasts small, firm-look-ing, the lips between her legs wetly glistening, her sex absolute-ly hairless.

"I ain't interested," said Rankin.

LuAnn leered mockingly at him.

"It never just does for me the way it ought to," Rankin told her.

"It never just does that way for nobody." Rearing back, LuAnn slapped his face, the sound reverberating in the car, as the effect of its pain to Rankin reverberated in his head. LuAnn slapped him again, splitting his lip. "Everybody comes at it different."

Rankin closed his eyes, in pain the more for looking at her.

He felt the sting of another slap, then another, against his cheek, the rush of blood to his groin. "Open your eyes, tough boy."

Rankin did, then opened his door, stepped out, strode around to the other door, opened it, and jerked LuAnn out of the car. He pushed her upper body face first onto the Tranny's hood, kicked her feet apart, forced open her cheeks, and went hard and deep into her. Buried in her, he saw, not in pictures, but in shades as dark as the crows now flocked in the tops of the trees ringing the church, the hideous creature the sons of bitches had made of Little Charlie and then he saw, in even darker colors, the horror Little Charlie had wrought (or Rankin had dreamed) last night.

* * *

Waking one morning to the memory of Little Charlie smash-ing a claw-hammer into Chester Rhimes's face as Rhimes, hours earlier, had slept next to Rankin's mother; Chester Rhimes screaming, groping at the hole where his right eye had been; lit-tle Charlie bashing him again, taking out Chester Rhimes's left eye; a third blow snapping Chester Rhimes's front teeth, shatter-

ing his jaw; Chester Rhimes, trying to cry, scream, beg, emitting only frothy blood bubbles; Little Charlie taking the hammer to Rankin's mother, still struggling awake; whacking her sixteen times (Little Charlie counting each blow aloud as he administered it) turning her features into formless red pulp; the twentieth and final blow (Little Charlie bringing the hammer down with all his strength from as high over his head as he could reach) crushing Chester Rhimes's Adam's apple to make him as mute as he'd once made Little Charlie.

Rankin, that morning ten years ago, believing he could smell their blood from where he lay.

How free, how powerful, he'd felt.

How deflated, how absolutely helpless, minutes later to hear them beyond their bedroom door fucking, arguing, showering, to see them come out of that room as alive and healthy as they'd ever been.

* * *

From his wallet he took a five spot, then tossed it into the air. He watched the bill land and, in the slight breeze, flutter across the lot toward the church.

In a thin stand of pines bordering an open field behind the swing holding him, a squirrel chattered, a cardinal chirped, a pine cone came to ground with a dull thud; two giant oaks facing him shuddered from the fluttery movements of the birds blackening them; a jet, in his eyes smaller than him, noiselessly spewed exhaust.

A spell is what he felt he was under, as if someone—Buddha, is who—owned a key to his mind and could unlock it when he wanted, could put into it thoughts, visions, dreams, could make Charlie Rankin act mad when he didn't want to be mad, act vicious when he wasn't vicious, see people he didn't know as people he did know, believe his niche was to be a cold-blooded killer when he didn't want to be a cold-blooded killer, when he wanted just to be rid of what in his head made him mad and vicious.

He emptied the beer he'd been drinking onto a small ant hill in the patch of worn dirt between his feet, wondering if the world would have been better off if he had slit Buddha's throat and gotten life for it than it was having Charlie Rankin out in it, running loose; he speculated that, the way he'd tapped into Charlie Rankin's recurring nightmares, the way he'd connected with Little Charlie, Buddha might be God and Satan at once. The church door opened.

Stepping into the doorway fifty feet left of him Florence waved at him to come to her.

Rankin shook his head.

"You should see this, Samson. Come on!"

Rankin pictured himself running through a maze of corpses after Little Charlie and Little Charlie running faster and faster, increasing the distance between them. "I told you already."

"If you're scared because you never been in one, Samson, forget it—it's just a quiet, peaceful spot. And beautiful."

"I'm not scared of anything in there. I've seen the sun shining through windows before."

"Not through windows like these."

Rankin glanced above her at the bell tower in the church's steeple, its metal flashing catching the sun, putting spots in his eyes. "You got no idea all I've seen."

"I can guess, though, a lot of what you ain't seen, which I'd say from fucking you"—Florence nodded at the Tranny's hood—"is not much of anything just for the beauty of it." Not angry, spiteful, hurtful, her tone was as matter-of-fact, thought Rankin, as that of the judge who, noting Rankin's history of petty lawlessness, had dropped five years on him.

Rankin said, "You didn't act to mind it much."

Florence took from behind her ear, then put in her mouth, a cigarette. "LuAnn likes it about any way. Or makes it look like she does." She lighted the cigarette with matches from her sweater pocket. "And, to please her man, Florence'd go along with whatever gets him off."

Rankin abruptly stood up. "All of it fit together better inside."

"What all you talking about?"

"How I was gonna get on top a things when I got out."

"Once you're dead, living'll likely make more sense too."

"I hope to hell so. It don't now."

"Do you believe you got a soul, Samson?"

"I don't know if I do."

"You do. And a good one. It ain't old, though, like mine. It's young. I know about things like that."

"This con I said about before—Charlie Rankin"—Rankin eyed a hawk flying circles above the church—"he'd look in the mirror and see nothing but the air the rest a the world walks, talks, blows smoke, shits, and pisses in. Until Buddha finally made him see himself in it."

"What'd he look like to himself?"

Rankin walked at her. "A guy due something back from this world."

"Due what exactly?"

Rankin stopped before her, capturing under his right boot toe his five-dollar bill, picturing Little Charlie strangling that woman on the horse, the way he saw it now to get her attention, to get her to see him. He told Florence, "You'd be smart to get clear a me."

"I wasn't born smart, and I hear it don't come to you later."

Rankin ground his foot into the bill, saying, "If you're right on me having a soul, it's nothing against how wrong you are on it being a good one."

"I'd say my take on it, given how mixed up you are, is at least as good as yours."

Rankin's insides began to tremble. He was reacquainted with a feeling as if something alive and dangerous and too big for the space holding it was pulsing in him, wanting out of him. Struggling to contain the thing, he deliberately crouched down, slipped the bill from beneath his foot, and got back to his feet, experiencing the sun, in its many reflections, as a dagger trying to penetrate to the blackness at his center. Having no idea why, he handed the bill to Florence.

She looked oddly at it. "What did you moosh it for?"

Rankin's trembling externalized, affecting his fingers, then his right cheek, and the eye above it; the feeling in his stomach intensified. He clutched his hands to his mid-section, groaning. Florence wrapped an arm around him. "Come inside with me and take a blow," she said, leading him across the short space to the church's back door. "It's a great place to. You'll see."

* * *

A sense that the air, as still as it was, had been frozen; a weighty, substantial feel to his body, contributed to by the resounding of his footfalls on the wood floor; a sensation similar to what he'd felt (petrified over being caught and grateful for the attention paid him by a nice lady cop who gave him a Mars Bar while transporting him downtown) being apprehended red-handed breaking into a parked car, at the age of eleven his first arrest.

They sat on a pew in the middle of the chapel.

The multi-colored windows to either side of them etched with stars, a manger scene, old, bearded guys seemingly studying on them, a moon shooting exaggerated beams, a kneeling crowd, their heads bowed, their hands upraised at a face (God's face, guessed Rankin) in the sky.

The entering light, through the dyed glass, at once muted and magnified.

Rankin remembered his mother declaring (though she'd never gotten around to doing it) that someday she'd have them both baptized, this after attending with Rankin their one Communion Service, at which it was explained to them that only those cleansed of original sin (unlike the two of them) were meant to partake of the bread and grape juice circulating.

Paintings on the walls of angels, hard-looking cases laboring to hoist upright an empty cross, a man crying over another man's severed head in his lap, the Virgin Mary, stern-faced and beautiful, Jesus lifting a wine goblet above several men sitting at a long rectangular table, a small gang rolling a rock away from a cave's entrance.

On the hardwood pulpit, an open Bible, a chalice, a microphone; behind it a life-sized depiction of the Cross with Jesus on it, bleeding from His hands and feet, sores covering His body, gashes on His cheeks, His head lolling to one side, His eyes wide open, hurting beyond belief before the world, the pain showing in His every fiber.

Rankin imagining that his guts were growing too big for his body from eating him from the inside out, that he was getting nauseous on his own flesh. The quietness, more complete than any quietness he could remember, as if the room were the belly of a giant creature holding its breath around him, magnifying his own bodily sounds, his breathing, swallowing, blinking, inward churning. "The things He went through."

Rankin experienced Florence's voice as a shout reaching him through the flesh he imagined imprisoning him. He looked at her.

She shook her head before the Crucifixion scene. "For the likes of us."

"Someone good enough at it"—Rankin, scarcely aware he was speaking, heard his own voice struggling to make it through the same barrier hers had reached him through—"can convince you of anything you always halfway wanted to be true."

"You talking about preachers?"

"I don't know no preachers."

"Who you talking about then?"

"Maybe I dreamed it all what happened. I hope I dreamed it all."

"What do you hoped you dreamed, Samson?"

Rankin, instead of answering her, clutched again at his midsection that suddenly felt as if it would explode. Florence draped an arm around his shoulders. "Take some deep breaths, then let 'em out slow."

Rankin did as she told him to, and felt somewhat better, though he still had the sensation that something inside of him was expanding by devouring him.

"You ain't ate all day." Florence wiped sweat from his brow. "That must be the problem. Or else you're coming down with something."

Rankin raised his eyes to Jesus on the Cross.

"What proof you got of Him?"

"I got nothing without what I feel. I feel Him, Samson, like I feel your good soul."

"What's He feel like?"

"When I feel Him best, He feels like love, not the kind between a man and a woman, but the kind that's got nothing to do with sex."

"What's that feel like?"

Florence looked at him sadly. "You ought to get down on your knees, Samson, and ask Him to put some of it into you, to show you how it feels."

She grasped him at the elbow, got him to kneel down with her between the pews, Rankin feeling in her grip like a small child pulled from a body of water he'd swallowed a gut-full of. "Talk to Him, Samson."

"What about?"

"Tell Him you haven't got an appetite and that your stomach hurts and why it hurts and ask Him what to do to make it stop hurting."

"I don't know why it hurts."

"He can spot a kernel of bullshit, Samson, in a cornfield."

"My whole life, what I remember of it"—Rankin felt as if he were but a bodiless voice floating inside of the huge creature he pictured as having swallowed him—"I've had urges to hurt and kill people and been dreaming realer than life dreams I was doing it. When I was a kid the dreams would make me feel better till I woke up." He closed his eyes. "They were my secret. Then I told Buddha about them."

"Now tell God, Samson, it ain't your dreams that are giving you a bellyache"—her voice more discarnate words mingling with his inside the creature's belly—"tell Him you can't figure out how you could of dreamed coming by the money you're holding and those cuts on your face and your sore back."

Rankin opened his eyes.

"Tell Him, not me, Samson. Tell Him how your belly—your whole self—pains so much that if not for your fear of burning in hell for all the bad you've done you'd kill yourself to stop hurting."

He looked at Florence, recollecting that he was on his knees with her in a church and that he hardly knew her and wondering why she seemed to know so much about him and was angling to learn even more and how much already Rankin had told her. He said, "You ain't but a Bible thumper."

Florence laughed. "All you seen from me in scarcely a day? I know where to turn at near the end of my rope's all, Samson, and it ain't to anyone walking and talking."

"Nobody's giving two shits for you up there"—Rankin aimed his chin at the ceiling—"or you wouldn't be making porno movies."

"Up there"—Florence rolled her head in a circle—"in here. Out in the streets. He's everywhere, and He's all right with what I do, Samson, 'cause I ain't hurt nobody and I live just fine with myself unlike someone I know can't hardly stand it in their own skin."

Rankin grabbed her arm nearest him. "You bring up my dreams again you'll find out exactly who's been dreaming 'em."

"I didn't bring 'em up. You brought 'em up."

"See how little He helps you you open your mouth about 'em to anybody."

"Who besides God would want to hear 'em?"

Rankin dropped her arm. "I asked your Friend for a few things—when I was younger, I did." He stood up. "Not a damn thing come of it, and here I am."

He took off for the church's rear exit, aware of a rapid clattering from beyond it, Florence calling calmly after him, "He don't always answer you in my experience, Samson, when or in the way you think He will."

"He never answered me at all," Rankin hollered.

He opened the door.

Cantering across the paved parking lot toward the hardwood stand behind it was the horse, under the blonde woman, they'd passed miles ago out on the highway.

Rankin fell to his knees, trembling.

He watched from the doorway horse and rider enter a dirt path into the woods, from trees all around them hundreds of black birds rising up, squawking. At where she'd come up behind him, Florence touched softly the top of his head. She said, "Didn't they make good time."

* * *

"Months after I heard he was dead I kept seeing my daddy places—in a movie line, climbing on a bus, rollerblading past my school—until finally I caught up with him leaving a Big K-Mart, loaded down with bags, and told him 'you fucked up the worst not getting to know me, who would of changed your mind about splattering your brains.'" She opened her window, flicked out her dead cigarette.

"By then I knew the guy wasn't my daddy and that in my heart I'd known it all along, so I helped him pick up his purchases I'd spooked him into dropping and explained what the deal had been and he was real nice about it and even wrote down his phone number and told me if I wanted to talk on it more to call him anytime, but I never did want to talk on it more or to call him and I didn't either again mistake my daddy for being above ground."

"I ought to get shed of you," said Rankin.

"Just you's stopping you from it."

"It don't make sense I ain't."

Florence rolled up her window. "No more than it does I didn't send you packing the second I seen the shape a you this morning."

"You should have for sure. I don't know why you didn't."

That horse riding woman last night suddenly staring right at Little Charlie under his disguise, telling him "it's got a full tank of gas," accusing him with her eyes (Little Charlie's Mother's eyes) of being worse than every son of a bitch she'd never protected him from.

"What I think, Samson, we both know, without wholly knowing we know, that we connected big time, and that don't happen often—two people connecting over things in 'em only He can see."

Little Charlie enraged by what was in those eyes, Little Charlie deciding to fix it so those eyes would never find him again.

Rankin took an exit for downtown, telling himself Charlie Rankin hadn't killed or hurt no one, he hadn't had but a bad dream.

"It might be love."

He shot a glance at Florence.

She nodded to him. "What we got, might be. We'll see."

Rankin scowled at her.

Florence laughed. "You want to go bowling?"

"Why would I?"

Florence pulled a fresh smoke from her purse. "To relax that's why. To help you get straight in your mind what to do to get rid of the pain in your belly, and then you can go do it, so you'll want to eat again and won't be afraid to die for fear of burning in hell."

"I believe you might be loony. I don't know why I didn't see it before."

Florence lit up again. "You don't mean half what you say, Samson. You're turned inside out is all."

"I don't want to go bowling. You can count on that."

"Have you ever?"

"No."

"What fun things have you done, Samson—or let me put it this way—what's the funnest thing you've done?"

"I don't know—maybe driving fast as hell on a narrow, twisty road."

"That's it? Christ. What a cheap thrill."

"One time when I was a kid, I ran away from my mother and her boyfriend and spent three days in some woods by myself, eating berries and trying to finger fish out of a stream and carving all sorts of things from branches. There weren't another person around and at night I'd lay there, looking up at the moon through the trees, trying to guess at the sounds in the dark."

"Was you just ready to piss from fear? I'd a been."

"Not a bit." A strange sensation welled up in Rankin, one he'd not experienced in so long he scarcely remembered he ever had experienced it; he pushed at his eyes, hoping Florence wouldn't notice him at it. "I can't recollect a time, before or since, I been less afraid than I was then, knowing not a human being was in earshot of me. I might be there still but for a fisherman coming onto me and calling the state, as I weren't but ten and looked younger."

Rankin stopped the car at a red light. A sweeper truck went by so close to them the Tranny shook; a three-legged dog darted into traffic, then backed out again; a horn honking rhythmically formed in Rankin's mind a picture of a man bad hurt, yelling, "Help me! Help me!"

Florence, leaning across the seat, kissed Rankin's cheek, her scent suggesting a smoldering fire in a field of spring flowers.

"You might be dead wrong," said Rankin, "on what you think you see in me."

Florence reclined against her door, smoking, studying on him.

Rankin wondered if he'd ever had the ability to isolate a single, clear thought. He said, "If only I'd met you yesterday and gotten out of jail today."

Florence blew smoke slowly up at the ceiling.

Rankin had an urge to scream at her to quit acting so relaxed, to understand she, like he, could be obliterated in the next instant. Instead he told her, "I believe I'm too late to get on board with God. I'm pretty sure He wouldn't clear my slate if I asked Him to."

"Or you're pretty sure that He might and that you won't let Him."

"I ain't even sure all what's on it."

"Best thing, in the telling of it, would be to err to the bad side—to include on it even your dreams."

"I ain't, either, gonna go back to jail."

"Do I look to you like a cop?"

"Just don't tell me no more what I got to do."

"It's you driving. I'm just sitting here."

"I don't want to go into no more churches."

"You're the one got a bellyache on the way to taking me out to dinner."

"I think I'm going to give away what of the money I got left. Just hand it out to people in the street."

Florence shrugged. "It's in you, Samson, to make love to me a whole lot nicer and gentler than what you did with LuAnn on the hood of this car in broad daylight for just anyone walking by to see. That's what I'm waiting on."

"There is damn straight something off in you."

Florence nodded through the windshield. "Green light."

Rankin put the car in gear. He turned it to the right, toward the Sinclair.

* * *

Holding in his hand during a driving ice storm a nickel-plated .38 revolver equipped with a silencer, thinking that this is what the world had prepared him for, that of all the niches that might have been his, here was the one he would finally fit into.

"Shit, Samson!"

He looked up to see he'd run the Tranny onto the sidewalk, knocking over a trash bin.

"And you without a license," said Florence.

Breathing heavily, he backed up and parked the car at the curb. A puffer in high-water bellbottoms and a skull cap sissy-walked out of the Sinclair's revolving front door right of them. Goose-stepping pigeons scattered on the sidewalk. A near-hairless mutt, pinching a loaf as it ran, cut down an alley away from a red-haired black kid chasing it. Rankin turned to Florence, who'd touched his arm a second, or several seconds, earlier. "I gotta go see a guy in here I don't trust above the bottoms of his feet."

"What do you got to see him for?"

"To check out of a room he rented me."

"You ain't got to see him then. You got to get your stuff from the room he rented you and clear out."

"And I need to see how he acts seeing me."

Florence placed a finger on the bruise between his eyes. "Did he get you into the business that caused you this?"

Rankin shook his head. "He knows something about it though."

"Was he there?"

"Where?"

"Wherever it happened?"

"He couldn't a been. No."

"Then how could he know more about it than you do, Samson"—Florence applied gentle pressure to where she was touching him; Rankin, closing his eyes, remembered a guy looking up from a chair near a lighted fireplace, through a glass window, at Rankin peering in at him from out in the hail and a feeling that Charlie Rankin had fucked up again just by being alive—"who was there?"

A God-awful braying in the dark: staring into blackness in which shapes weren't who or what they seemed to be; Chester Rhimes attacking him with a piece of firewood; Little Charlie scared as hell.

"Do you dance, Samson?"

He opened his eyes to find Florence with her hands now in her lap, cradling a little .22 automatic. "You know"—she moved her feet in a slow gambol on the floorboards—"like this."

"I never have."

"It's sad how many fun things you ain't done. I could teach you how to, so that if it ever comes up that you have to you can."

"I can't see how it ever will come up."

"Nobody knows the future, Samson. Take me into your room and let me teach you. I could help you pack too. And maybe we could lay on the bed and watch a movie before you check out."

"I ain't the guy you keep mistaking me for. I'm either the worst son of bitch living or I'm loonier than you."

Florence, acting not to have heard him, pulled out the .22's clip, counted the six bullets in it, shoved it back into the gun. "And I'd like to see your personal belongings, what things you treasure most, so that if I decide to I'll know the sort of gift to buy you."

"I don't carry with me but a change of clothes."

"That'll make it easy to decide then."

"It's a wonder to me you've lived this long reckless way you go about it."

"I'd sooner not live at all than to live how you do, Samson, not trusting a soul, not even the one inside you." She raised and aimed the pistol at the spot on Rankin's forehead her finger had recently been pressing on; Rankin, coolly anticipating the bullet shredding his brain and a trap door opening beneath him, didn't even flinch. "I carry this against totally bad to the bone people. Do you believe I ain't encountered none yet?"

"I believe you won't know you have till it's too late."

"The evil in people looks into me and goes gentle as a lap dog. I don't know what causes it—something passing from Him through me maybe and speaking only to it through my eyes."

Rankin shrugged. "Good thing for you to tote that pistol case you're wrong."

Florence lowered the .22. "I wanted you to see it was loaded"—she tossed him the gun—"before I gave it to you."

Rankin shook his head, then chinpointed to the Sinclair. "I got a knife to deal with this guy it comes to it."

"Well I ain't got a knife and, in my present company"—Florence stared hard at him—"I still don't need it."

Rankin took her purse from her lap, stuck the gun in it, lay the purse back on her legs. He handed her his room key. "You go up ahead a me and pack my stuff, bring it down the lobby. I'll learn from you to dance another time."

* * *

A vomit-mopped-up-with-Mr. Clean smell; a workman, neck-deep in the busted elevator's shaft, whistling "Where Have You Gone Bill Bailey"; footsteps resounding on the enclosed metal stairs; two cops, coming out of the lunchroom, arguing over whether a local zoo lion should be put to death for mauling an escaped mental patient who'd vaulted into its compound; a bag lady, her hand out on a sunken couch she looked to have spent her life being pounded into, begging for charity in a hoarse whisper that unearthed in Rankin a picture of that strangled woman at the golf course house in a piss-soaked nightgown making a sound like a donkey's bray up at Little Charlie.

"Where's the little Spanish guy runs it?" Rankin asked the woman, nodding past her at the unoccupied cubicle housing the hotel's register.

The old bag gazed at him as if he were flecks of dust in the air.

Rankin took from his wallet and put into the crone's outstretched palm a hundred dollar bill; without looking at it she slipped the cash into a gymbag with a busted zipper between her feet.

Little Charlie sleeping naked in his mother's bed beneath a headboard supporting a glass jar of paper money (mostly twenties and fifties) dropped into it by a succession of strange mens grubby fingers.

"Buy you some shoes with it," Rankin told the woman, noting her tattered bedroom slippers.

The woman closed her eyes.

In the several seconds Rankin stood above her hoping she'd reopen them and smile and/or look kindly at him, she didn't. "That was a hundred bucks," he said.

The woman started to snore.

Rankin approached the register.

* * *

In the cubicle's rear wall a half-glass door exposed a small room containing a metal table at which Ornay Corale, eating a sandwich, played cards with a solid-built guy.

Rankin couldn't put a finger on what in the second guy's appearance increased his edginess over revisiting the Sinclair.

He pushed the help buzzer in the partition separating the cubicle from the lobby.

Corale, glancing up, waved to him from behind the glass in the way of a driver apologizing to another driver for cutting him off in traffic; then he lay down his cards, stood, strode to the door, yanked a shade down over the pane in its upper portion; he stepped out of the room, shutting the door behind him. "Told you, didn't I, Charlie, that snow'd amount to a dry fart?"

Rankin responded to the little deskman only by ringing the buzzer again.

Corale hooted out a lungful of smoke. "I know you ain't here 'cause your bed needs changing, Charlie"—walking at the partition, he swiped from his shirt front ash dropped from a cigarette gone near to its filter in one corner of his lips—"account my maid tells me it ain't been slept in."

Rankin mutely pressed the buzzer a third time.

Corale, grinning uncomfortably, picked with a fingernail at his teeth nearest his cigarette. "I'll put you down, Charlie, for another night?"

Rankin shook his head.

Corale came to an abrupt stop a good arm's length yet from the partition. "You're leaving us, Charlie?"

Rankin nodded.

"You sure?" Corale laughed too loud. "So soon, I mean?"

Rankin leaned in at the deskman, whiffing from him onions, rank smoke, a shit cologne. "Why would I stay longer?"

Corale scanned the lobby only the old bag and the elevator repairman currently occupied. "You're asking me, Charlie?"

"I won't a second time."

"It's your business, not mine, brought you here, Charlie. Why would I know about your business?"

"Knowing my business, deskman, is your business."

Corale with two fingers fished the butt from between his lips. "I'm 'bout the last one to hear anything, Charlie."

Rankin took hold of and wadded up Corale's shirt front with one hand.

"I'm just a pissant, Charlie, gets thrown a coupla bucks once in a while to make sure certain people—Charlie Rankin for one—have what they need—"

"Our boss who throws 'em to ya got a problem with me checking out when I want to?"

Trying to put the cigarette back in his mouth, Corale banged it against his lip and dropped it. He hissed, "I don't know what you're doing here talking to me, Charlie! You got the room you was supposed to get. Something wrong?"

Rankin twisted the fabric in his right hand, whispering, "You tell me if there is, Ornay."

Corale viewed nervously the lobby. "What do you think, Charlie—Mr. Pettigrew gets word a certain guy shows up for work this morning like he always has after you and Mr. Pettigrew had an arrangement?"

Rankin let go of Corale's shirt.

"Mr. Pettigrew's gonna want to know if I've seen you, Charlie."

Rankin, backing away from the partition, touched, as if blindly groping a stranger's body, two fingers to the Band-Aids on his nose, to the bruise between his eyes, to the scratches on his forearms.

"Do you want me to tell him anything?"

Rankin stared uncomprehendingly at the deskman.

"You know, like shit happened, and tomorrow's another day?"

Chester Rhimes's face turning purple above Little Charlie's clenched fingers around his neck.

"The exact shit that happened won't matter to him, he don't even have to hear it"—Corale skittishly squatted, picked up his cigarette, fit the tiny nub back between his lips; he straightened up, eyeing Rankin as if Rankin were an animal mad with rabies—"only that you said for me to tell him that the certain guy won't be at work tomorrow morning."

Rankin remembered Little Charlie one night snapping his fingers and becoming Poof Man and waking up in daylight, covered in blood, recalling punches, knife blades, bullets passing harmlessly through him. "Shit happened," he said, with the sensation that he was dreaming as he stood there of a time when he'd been awake.

"And tomorrow's another day?"

"Yeah."

"I'll tell him, Charlie—put his mind at ease."

Florence came out of the stairway door dangling Rankin's sailor's bag over one shoulder. Against Rankin's instructions to her to not let on in the Sinclair she knew him, she strode through the lobby to him. She handed him his room key. "I didn't need it"—she glared at the deskman—"account a girl was up there going through my man's clothes."

The butt he'd just placed back between his lips again falling from them Corale said, "Goddamn maid. I'll have her ass for it."

"I saw her good enough in the second 'fore she lit out like a burglar"—Florence made a one-handed whisking motion at the street—"to know she weren't in a maid's get-up." She looked at Rankin. "You're not keeping company with another blonde's young as me?"

Rankin shook his head to her in the same instant that he put an identity to Ornay Corale's card partner. He dropped the key onto the partition in front of Corale. He told Florence, "Go out the car. I'll be along directly."

For a few seconds Florence appeared undecided on her next move. Then she left, toting Rankin's belongings.

Rankin watched her disappear through the circular glass exit. He turned back to Ornay Corale.

Fumbling in his shirt pocket for a fresh smoke the deskman backed steadily toward the adjoining room. Rankin vaulted over the partition, wrapped his left arm around Corale's neck, opened the door to the rear room, dragged Corale into the room, and shut the door. The pretty boy who, with the blonde girl, had tried to rob Rankin at the bus station lockers yesterday leapt up from the table. Before the guy could get out whatever he was reaching for in the rear of his pants-waist, Rankin had the blade of his gravity knife pressed to Ornay Corale's throat. "I got a breathing condition, Charlie"—Corale wheezed—"a nervous thing . . . !"

"Did you reckon I'd left a forwarding address in my room, Ornay? Or was you having the girl toss it chancing I'd been stupid enough to stash the cash in it?"

"She was only hunting anything might give us a line to you, Charlie, on account—you know—Mr. Pettigrew, he didn't know if you'd split with his money without ya'd earned it, but that was a misunderstanding, right, Charlie?—tomorrow's another day?—that's what I'm going to tell him."

"That had to be your play at the bus station, Ornay. Buddha wouldn't set me up to steal from me his own money. If he'd had wind of it you two and the girl wouldn't be breathing."

"I'm not following you, Charlie. What bus station?"

Rankin had the sensation his life was a movie being played backward, highlighting parts of it he'd already lived in a whole different light. He remembered, a day and a half ago, on his way to locker #102, being ready—eager—to kill someone (he didn't care who), convinced a killer is what he was meant to be. He had a terrible feeling the bad person he was now had scraped and crawled his way out of the skin of a person far worse than him. His fingers around the knife shook. "Charlie, please—for fuck sake let me get at my inhaler."

Rankin angled his head at the pretty boy. "Looks as if I'm in the spot I'd been in if you'd done better robbing me."

The guy said, "This is the first time I've laid eyes on you, Mister."

Rankin said, "Everybody lies," blinking, unsure now if this was or wasn't the grab-and-run guy.

The guy shrugged. "Still I ain't who you think I am. You've mistaken me for somebody else."

"You've mistaken us both, all three of us, the fucking maid too"—Corale gasped—"for other people, Charlie."

"Don't call me that no more."

"Don't call you Charlie?"

"Tell him—tell Buddha—not to no more neither."

"Okay."

"And tell him he don't know me from any other caged animal he hypnotized and sweet-talked into fucking him up the ass." He pushed Corale into the arms of the other guy. Then he put away his knife and left, on his way out taking from his wallet another C-note and slipping it into a pocket of the tattered raincoat being worn by the old bag snoring on the lobby couch.

* * *

A fear that just outside the area he'd spent the last two days in the earth ended without warning in a depthless black void kept him from getting as far gone as fast as he could from where he was at.

He cruised four times through the same several blocks, wondering if everything he thought he was seeing—people, buildings, vehicles—existed only (like maybe the murders he'd recalled Little Charlie committing) in his mind. He stopped the Tranny finally in a neighborhood much like the one they'd come from, trusting nothing, not even that he'd not already driven off the end of the earth, into a hell indistinguishable from the life he'd hoped death would save him from. Unaware of thinking or forming the words, he said, "When I was a kid I heard if you stared straight at the sun long enough you'd go blind, so I tried it, but it hurt so much I quit doing it while I was still seeing."

"What in the world'd you want to go blind for?"

"All I remember—I didn't like what I was looking at."

"So why didn't you look at something besides it?"

"It was everything I could see."

Florence said, "Once I seen two kids in the street stone to death a pretty Persian cat that must have got away from its owner and that night I woke up crying for the ones who'd killed it because between them and it, they was by far the worse off."

"What the fuck are you telling me about a dead cat and two asshole kids for?"

"I thought we was sharing our earliest memories."

Rankin turned off the ignition. He opened his window, hearing, with the impression they were being orchestrated to tell him something (he couldn't decipher what), honking horns, disembodied shouts, whirring tires, a jackhammer he imagined as being applied to his brain, shredding his already disconnected thoughts into images, memories, wisps of near and long ago nightmares.

"You didn't want to get a rub, you didn't want to have a picnic, you didn't want to go to the zoo, you didn't want to bowl, you didn't want to watch a movie"—Florence's voice reached him as a distinct sound in that din—"it's looking more and more like you don't want to go out to dinner."

Rankin faced her.

She nodded across the intersection past him, at Randy's Watering Hole. "Maybe we could have a few drinks and play pool while you're working up to doing what you're going to have to do to get your appetite back and you into His good graces."

Rankin took the key from the ignition; he put it in his pocket. Opening his door, he said, "If the place has even got a table."

* * *

The chunky, Mexican bartender (he had Z carved into his right cheek and hair thick as kelp) believed he'd worked with Rankin. "Four years ago on a non-union crew putting a bridge over Roos Gap up in San Lee County?"

Rankin shook his head.

"Jesus, yes." The bartender put down in front of Rankin his Bud and Wild Turkey order. "You drove a red El Camino with a black racing stripe and weren't five feet from me when that Indian kid from Canada—we called him Chief and he couldn't been but nineteen—hit the rocks from three hundred feet up after losing it on a beam wet with dew."

Rankin wordlessly downed the Turkey, put the glass on the bar, gazed into the mirror at the reflection of Florence, adding a quarter to the rail of the pool table in the far corner, jawing with one of the shooters, a stringbean without muscles, in a muscle shirt, his razored scalp halved lengthwise by old stitch marks.

"You got a good-looking, nice as can be wife—or had one—and two kids?"

"Never been married. Never been on a bridge job." Less than a dozen shadowy figures in the semi-darkness drinking, moving about, "Stairway to Heaven" on the juke, pool balls clacking, laughter, a stale, boozy smell, floating smoke clouds dense as thunder heads, Rankin trying to imagine having a bridge job (any kind of job), a nice as could be wife (any sort of wife), two kids, a home, his anger building, without him conscious of why, at this gabby Mex who'd made him see so starkly the life he was in by causing him to picture himself, if only fleetingly, in the far better sounding life of the guy he'd been mistaken for. The bartender rapped his knuckles twice on the bar.

"The shot and chaser are on the house, my man."

Rankin picked up his beer. He took a deep breath, exhaled it slow (weird, he thought, he remembered a worthless little thing like this breathing technique taught to him by a jail shrink to supposedly keep a lid on his rage when it started to boil and other things, whole parts of his life, he remembered, if at all, only sketchily or in dreams).

"Seeing that kid with all them unlived years dropping like a shot bird through the air"—the bartender made a grave frown—"man, it ruined me. I couldn't go up ten feet after that without I'd start to shake."

"I never seen it," said Rankin. "I wasn't there."

The bartender shrugged as if it didn't matter to him if or not Rankin had seen it, if or not he'd been there, if or not he was who the Mex had said he was. "I quit so not to be fired and pretty soon I started to get pissed off at my wife and kids for looking at me as if I was half the size I used to be—though I realized later I'd shrunk only in my eyes—plus I couldn't find other work to fit me and the shit jobs, like this one, I took just to be employed didn't bring home near what steelwork had and my wife hung in awhile, till she saw and I saw things had changed for good, then she took off with my four babies out west and I've seen 'em exactly twice since."

Rankin stood and turned his back to the bar, abruptly realizing that since he'd woken up that morning he'd had no imagined picture of himself; even when he'd caught his reflection in a window or mirror he'd looked right through or beyond himself as if he were passing Charlie Rankin in a crowd; also that he couldn't recall the sound of his voice from before he started talking to Florence earlier that day.

He heard at his back the bartender tell him, "I can still hear him screaming as he fell, seemed like for five minutes or more it went on. I hardly knew the kid and I ain't been able to shake it, man."

Rankin walked away from the Mex, into the men's toilet. He shut the door; moaning, he grabbed his stomach, in which he felt a sporadic pulsing, as if from tiny, rock-hard fists internally pummeling him. His mind's eye showed him Little Charlie, against Chester Rhimes's wallops, holding his breath until he blacked out laughing inside at the son of a bitch for never having succeeded in forcing a sound from him, then (minutes, hours, days, years later?) opening his eyes to find his mother atop him, breathing heatedly in her efforts to love him.

No. Not his mother.

And Little Charlie wasn't lying under her; he was sitting atop her, as she uttered gasping, croaking sounds through a crushed larynx and stared wild eyed up into four dark, gaping holes in his otherwise blank face.

Rankin reached up and touched a finger to his eyes, his nose, his mouth.

He remembered in that moment buying, with his new boots and gloves, a black ski mask, the clerk he'd bought it from remarking, "You must be expecting the real deal."

Buddha declaring that a diamond, no matter how deeply buried in the earth, is a diamond, that one's dreams, even if they are nightmares, are the purest part of one's self.

He stumbled to the sink; he splashed water onto his face, picturing abstractly, as if he were imagining the faces of people with whom he'd been trapped in a dark room, the loneliness of prison, the desolation of anonymity, the desperation to be seen by another set of human eyes, to be touched by caring hands, to be felt by a warm body.

He remembered pulling the mask onto his head like a watch cap, reminding himself to yank it down later over his features.

He pulled a towel from the wall rack, dried his face; he dropped the towel in the trash, remembering as he did so tossing into a gas station dumpster the night before a duffel bag holding the bloody mask, gloves, the clothes he'd worn from prison, and a .38 revolver, and he remembered exactly where that dumpster was.

He reentered the room to find Florence gone.

* * *

Against his mental picture of her, the bar's occupants struck him as fleshly offspring of the same ghost; he perceived them as one person in different bodies, using different voices, a single son of a bitch eyeing from every angle Charlie Rankin approaching the pool table. A cue stick was thrust out at him.

The spindly guy holding it inquired of him, "Five bucks a game rich enough for an assassin like you?"

Rankin perceived himself in that moment as someone a smart person would go miles to avoid; he imagined a part of him, at odds with the rest of him, wriggling to escape his own grip. He pointed to his chest. "You think you know me?"

The guy sighted along the length of the cue at him. "Ain't you the money shooter?"

"Ain't I what?"

"Delilah had it you was the one of the two of you to watch out for."

Rankin pictured countless closed doors encircling him, each one opening onto a human face that recognized him in a form no other face recognized him in, that remembered him from a place no other face remembered him from, the faces together witnesses to every moment Charlie Rankin had lived or dreamed he'd lived. He said, "I don't know no Delilah."

A tub of lard in denim overalls standing near the first guy said, "He's fucking with you, Samson."

Rankin shifted his eyes to the tub of lard.

The guy grinned, his yellow teeth, behind matted facial hair, bringing to Rankin's mind a jackal's fangs. "She didn't tell us her name."

"Only your name, Samson," said the spindly guy.

Rankin took from the spindly guy the cue; he envisioned busting the cue over the guy's head, the blow not altering the guy's appearance, the cue being stopped only by a wall or the floor after passing through thin air. "Where is she?"

"Delilah?"

Rankin tightened his grip on the cue. "Florence. Her name's Florence."

The tub of lard nodded down a hallway left of him; indenting his right nostril with an index finger, he inhaled exaggeratedly through his left one, as if taking something up into it.

The first guy said, "You want to go 'head break, Samson, or wait for her?"

Rankin, not answering, carrying the stick still, strided past the table, into the hallway; darker even than the bar, it contained two closed doors, several feet apart, in its right wall; an emergency exit filled its far end. Next to the first door, marked STORAGE, Rankin stopped, then put an ear to its wood facing; indistinct noises reached him; he seized and twisted the door's handle; he pushed it open.

The stringbean with stitch marks on his head jumped back, colliding with the boxes, stacked along the far wall, against which he'd been pinning Florence, her sweater yanked up over her face, his hand tearing at her panties, his hard-on jabbing at her mid-section. "What the fuck, man?"

Florence, panting heavily, yanked down her sweater; she spit on the floor, running a hand back through her hair.

The guy struggled to rezip his pants.

Rankin stepped into the room.

Raising his hands before him, Stitch Marks made as if to back up through the boxes. "Lose the cue, okay, man?"

Rankin shut the door.

"This was up to your lady, man. I don't go around soliciting people to give shit away to, believe it or not."

A bare ceiling bulb (the room's only light) cast on the floor an expanded shadow of Florence, her head lowered, swiping at her mouth, pushing a fist into her eyes, her make-up smeared, her lower lip bleeding. Certain when he couldn't find her in the bar she'd run out on him, Rankin was caught off guard by his feeling at discovering she hadn't, a feeling telling him something good maybe existed in him because someone good maybe hadn't given up on him. He pushed the cue's point into Stitch Marks's chest.

Stitch Marks gyrated against the pressure. "She gets me in here, man—not the other way around, all right?—then gives me fifteen bucks for thirty's worth a beanies—what's a guy supposed to think?"

"I told you how much money I had"—Florence's voice suggested to Rankin a little girl, ten or so, talking to a pet dog she couldn't believe had bit her purposefully—"and for you to give me what it would pay for. I didn't say nothing about you raping me!"

Rankin lifted the stick to the top of the guy's skull. "What was it opened you up?"

The guy stared blankly at him.

Transfixed by a vision of a head being zippered open and things being removed from it, Rankin ran the cue's felt point along the keloid scars sectioning the guy's pate.

Stitch Marks wet his lips with his tongue. "Doctors," he told Rankin.

"Why did they?"

"A part a my brain woulda killed me they hadn't got it out."

"What all'd they take out with it?"

"What do you mean?"

"Did they take out your nightmares? Your memories? All them fucked up thoughts won't let a man live peaceful?"

"After they took out whatever they took out, man, I woke up not remembering what was gone and mostly glad of it."

"They took all that out it shoulda made you nicer, smarter, a better fucking human being. It would of me."

The guy made a nervous laugh.

Rankin jerked from off the guy's head, then jabbed hard into his stomach, the cue's point; the guy doubled up, groaning; Rankin whapped the stick against the back of the guy's neck; the guy fell to his knees, a voice in Rankin's head telling him it as well could be, it ought to be, Charlie Rankin getting clobbered. He raised up the stick again meaning to beat the guy senseless. Florence grabbed his arm.

Rankin looked at her; her eyes were wet; Rankin couldn't tell if she was crying. He smelled in the room (each of the odors as separate in his perception of them as each of his fingers were to his hand) something suggesting brine leaking from a busted pickle jar, a scent hinting at death (maybe ant or roach spray), Stitch Marks's sweaty, heated-up stench, Florence's perfume, half-masking the smell of her fear.

She took the stick from him.

Rankin looked back down at Stitch Marks, gasping, his flesh around his roseate scar the color of old bones.

"I was stupid," said Florence.

Little Charlie over that woman, her pushing against Little Charlie's hand in her hair, whispering, "Please stop."

"I'd a got through it—I've gotten through worse." Florence

smiled feebly at him, her lower lip slightly swollen. "Because of you I didn't have to." She kissed his cheek.

Rankin stepped uncomfortably away from her. "He hurt you much?"

She shook her head.

"People ain't as good's you think they are."

She nodded down at Stitch Marks. "I never thought he was much good. I only wanted to buy some buzz off'n him."

"As bad as he looks to you now, I'm a hundred times worse."

Florence held his face in her hands. "No, you ain't."

"You ain't got no power to see into nobody. Thinking you do'll only end you up in a bad place."

Florence didn't say anything.

Rankin had a sudden desire to wrap his arms around her, but could no more see himself doing it than he could see himself jumping to the moon. He said, "Where I'm going to from here, you don't want to go to. Believe me."

"Why don't I?"

Rankin kicked Stitch Marks viciously in the abdomen (not from anger, but to make Florence watch him do it and because he found it simpler to show her than to tell her why she didn't want to go with him even another second) Stitch Marks groaning, gripping his mid-section, falling onto his back.

Florence flinched.

Rankin stared hard at her. "And I think you got as good a idea as me where I'll likely end up for where I've been."

Florence made no response.

Rankin took the cue from her and tossed it atop the boxes.

"So, take care yourself better'n you have been. You deserve to."

He walked out of the room and turned left toward the emergency exit. He reached the exit and stopped, hearing footsteps behind him. He opened the door onto a garish sunset. He held the door open, not turning around, waiting for Florence to catch up with him, and to pass ahead of him into the dying day, Rankin feeling at once unaccountably blessed and deservedly cursed.

* * *

Wind whistled through the cracked open front windows; the radio disgorged country ballads; Florence's right foot moved on the floor in rhythm with her wagging head; the smoke from her cigarettes (lighted by her one from another) swirled in a cooling cross-draft.

Trying, on this road vaguely familiar to him, not to see past the Tranny's headlight beams (in the growing gloom, the dull shafts touched street signs, the backs of cars, trees, scattered buildings) Rankin remembered catching, with his bare hands, a twelve inch trout from a stream in those woods he'd run off into as a boy; he remembered cooking the fish over a fire and eating it, laughing aloud in the darkness from the good feeling it gave him.

Instinct and memory led him away from the city, back through Alto proper, onto a two lane highway derived from the town's main drag.

An unlighted tractor, suggesting a ghost ship on a fog-covered ocean, cut through a field to their left; on the gravel shoulder opposite it, a convertible carrying screaming teenagers sped past them. Rankin tried to recall, and couldn't, laughing anywhere again the way he'd laughed in those woods.

He glanced at Florence, facing him with her eyes closed; he imagined her seeing in her head, along with everything else about him she could see, a him no one saw when looking at him, a sliver of himself alive only in a secluded corner of his mind, a not such a bad Charlie Rankin she somehow (angel or sorceress that she was) had divulged.

On the road's shoulder, a guy hitchhiking stood as still as a statue beneath a high tension wire holding dozens of birds as static as him; in the murky field behind them a crane, looking like the illuminated arm of a half-concealed giant, raised a silo's domed top into the air; lost in her ballads, Florence gazed blindly at it all.

Rankin guessed that to be with him still, sensing what she did about him, she had to be more than a little off—unless in fact she was an angel or a sorceress. He remembered how she'd told him the good in her was more powerful than the bad in anyone else and how, after he'd stopped Stitch Marks from raping her, instead of wanting to see Stitch Marks get some of what he'd given her, she'd stopped Rankin from pummeling the guy.

Something about her frightened Rankin more than did any of the many violent people he knew and had known.

Something else about her (more powerful than whatever about her frightened him) aroused in him a warm feeling (it had not a thing to do with sex) nothing in his experience with people prepared him for.

Unable to find her after coming out of Randy's Watering Hole men's room, certain he'd seen her for the last time, he'd felt as if he'd been jettisoned into a cold, desolate outback inhabited by every son of a bitch he'd ever known or might have known, a place where to show warmth was akin to bleeding in a shark tank, sad, enraged, fucked over, obsessing on the sort of violence he remembered or dreamed Little Charlie committing, the way he'd felt (he realized it now) when he'd heard Full Boat was dead.

* * *

"I'm gonna find me another stray," said Florence.

Rankin turned to her, thinking she'd be looking at him; her eyes, though, hadn't opened.

"One, like the one that come to me last time out of the blue, that looks lonely and on death's door and I'll take this one in too and nurse it back to health and show it how nice it can be to be alive and in the company of good people."

Rankin became aware in that moment that darkness had arrived; it felt to him as if he'd brought it on with an eyeblink, a blink that had also jostled free something in his brain; a hum like the sound of a high-flying plane to those on the ground beneath it filled his ears; in his mind's eye he saw himself stepping from the driver's side of an idling car, toting under one arm a stuffed cloth sack; clouds of cool, visible dampness in the air; the bulbs of half-a-dozen pole lamps dully shining in blue halos around a paved parking lot; a woman cashier reading a magazine in a small glass-enclosed booth attached to a lighted building.

"And if this one dies too"—Florence faced the ceiling, as if making blind contact with someone in or beyond it—"well I'll miss it like I miss Gold, but at least I'll know it didn't leave this world, no more than Gold did, never having been loved by nobody in it."

Rankin didn't reply to her (he wasn't sure she was awake even).

He gazed upward through the windshield; stars and a crescent moon dimly perforated a sheen of papery clouds; a few days after he'd mentioned to Buddha that what he missed most in prison was a view of the night sky, how the sky at night was maybe his all time favorite sight, Buddha had beckoned him into his cell and told him to lie on his back on Buddha's bunk; Rankin did, to see, on the ceiling above the bed, a hand-drawn, luminescent mural of the heavens (every constellation and star positioned in it exactly where Rankin remembered them being in fact).

"Because the only thing I can still do for Gold," said Florence, "is to love another homeless cat as much as I did him."

Rankin wondering if he'd only done what he'd done in Buddha's bed all those times so that, after he'd done it, he could gaze up for a while at that painted sky, imagining he was lying alone beneath the real one, worlds from anyone, in those dark woods he'd run off into as a child.

"If I could bring in and love more than one of them at a time I would, but I can't seem to focus on more than one of 'em at once."

Rankin was getting spooked listening to her. "You still high on that shit?"

Her eyes opened at him. "This car's swaying side-to-side."

"The car ain't doing nothing."

"It feels like we're on the ocean in a little dingy."

"You're fucked up still is all."

"No. The wheels is out of balance or something."

Rankin remembered an owl hooing off in the blackness; the solid splash of his footsteps crossing the lot; a gasoline smell; six fuel pumps but no vehicle or person at them; a feeling as if in that fog-covered night he was the only thing of substance, as if everything else divulged by his senses was as ephemeral as a forgotten thought.

The heaviness of a metal dumpster's lid as he lifted it with one hand.

"There's the cause of it," said Florence.

He looked at her.

She nodded to his hands, shaking on the steering wheel, moving it, back and forth, in short jerks.

He squeezed the wheel, stopping the motion. "Another cat'd be lucky to have you," he told Florence.

"You making fun of me?"

"No."

"Did you hear me say something about a cat just now?"

"You said you was gonna get another one."

She nodded, as if he'd verified what she'd been wondering

about. "The truth is, loving one of 'em gives me at least as good a feeling as one of 'em gets being loved by me."

"How'd you end up being so good from being treated so bad?"

"I don't know what you mean."

Rankin shrugged. He imagined a wave forcefully breaking over him. His eyes fixated on a glowing, yellow Sunoco sign ahead of them. He heard in his mind a crash, louder than a gunshot, from the dumpster's lid closing after he'd dropped it. He put on the Tranny's right blinker. He told Florence, "We're here."

* * *

Half-a-dozen pumps under a lighted awning; a little grocery/food mart; a separate booth holding a girl gas clerk painting her fingernails; a scowling bald guy in combat fatigues fueling up a Ford Windstar packed with dogs and kids; two rednecks (brothers maybe) with billygoat beards, going with wrenches at a Ram Charger's exposed engine; a pretty woman, dressed nice, putting air in a Saab's tires; "Long Tall Sally" over someone's radio; gas fumes; cigar smoke; the dispensing whine of the pumps.

Rankin, circling the building slowly, picturing a zigzagging trail of all-night pit stops, any or all of which might have been the one he was now at, leading back to the day he'd left behind him for dead his Mother and Chester Rhimes.

"You've been here before." More a statement than a question from Florence.

In those first years of being on his own (from fourteen to maybe eighteen) jacking open concession machines for food, snatching unattended wallets, purses, coats, hats, car keys, briefcases, cleaning his teeth, dick, balls, ass, armpits in public cans, playing rest stop video games until he'd used up his quarters or

was made to leave the premises, sleeping on secluded patches of
grass or in stolen or borrowed cars.

"Was it last night you were here?"

Rankin didn't answer her. They rounded the building's left,
rear corner.

"What is it you're looking for, Samson?"

He saw it exactly where, in the same moment, he remembered it being; snug to the section of wall farthest, on that side,
from the store's front. He stopped the Tranny a ways past it,
then backed up to within five feet of it. He put the car in park,
directly facing the pumps. Florence took a cigarette out of her
sweater pocket; watching him, she lit it from the nub burning
in her mouth; she snubbed the nub out in the dash ashtray.
Rankin lowered his window completely. He gazed up into the
darkness, the engine's vibrations beneath him forming in his
mind a picture of someone pushing weakly against him in an
attempt to avoid suffocating under him. "How is it that in one
mirror a girl can look beautiful to herself and in another one
like a skinny-assed little junkie whore?"

He lowered his eyes to see Florence gazing into the vanity
mirror beneath her visor. "Do you think it's more the mirror or
what's in your mind when you're looking at it?"

Rankin didn't say.

Florence ran a tube of bright purple lipstick around her lips,
smacked her lips, then put the lipstick away. She faced Rankin
gravely. "Who do you see?"

"A girl who looks better than any girl I've ever seen."

"Not a skinny-assed little junkie whore?"

"No."

"This good-looking girl you're looking at named LuAnn?"

"Her name's Florence."

Florence nodded straight-faced to him. "You're not blowing
smoke up my ass?"

Rankin shook his head.

"Guess that must make you something special"—she pushed up the visor and reached for her door handle—"having a girl better than any girl you've ever seen choosing you, out of all the men living under the eyes of God, to fall for and believe in."

A baby started crying in the night, creating to Rankin a picture of that woman Little Charlie had strangled at the golf course house, gazing into an empty crib. He abruptly turned to the Tranny's rear window.

"Samson?"

He heard in his mind, while looking past the window at the dumpster (a blue metal box the Tranny's height and maybe half its length), the woman telling Little Charlie, "There isn't one."

"I'm going to look in it," he said.

"In the garbage bin?"

Rankin nodded.

"What for?"

"To know I ain't dreaming now."

Florence, showing no reaction to his answer and acting as if searching through a public dumpster was a normal activity, said, "Should I help you?"

Rankin shook his head.

"I'll go inside then." Florence opened her door and stepped out of the car. Rankin envisioned a person who looked just like him concealed in the darkness beyond the arc of the rest stop lights, watching her, as he was. In the cooling air, she hugged herself crossing the lot; her exhalations trailed her in white puffs; a line of near-naked saplings, clinging to the last of their leaves, stood left of her on the grass bordering the building, until she vanished around its front corner.

Rankin got out of the Tranny, as a woman carrying a baby appeared from where Florence had disappeared; the woman walked to a station wagon parked at the pumps, put the baby (Rankin guessed it was the one crying earlier, though for all the noise it was making now it might have been asleep or dead) into the rear seat, recalling to Rankin how Little Charlie had been transfixed by the neatness of that empty crib's freshly made sheets, the mobiles hanging above it, its sweet, powdery smell, the woman's soft hair like Little Charlie's mother's hair, her warm breasts—

The woman at the station wagon got in behind its wheel. She started up the car and drove off. Feeling as if he were in a narrowing corridor in which a third wall was forming to his rear, Rankin made his way to the dumpster (it stood directly under a pole light). He opened it; the bang its cover made landing on it was as familiar to him as the memory of punches hitting him.

Smells of gone milk, rotting vegetables, fast food, festering flesh.

He peered into the dumpster.

Five or six full trash bags partially hidden amid drink containers, hamburger cartons, Styrofoam coffee cups, a cat cadaver, its black and white head, streaming with maggots, grotesquely misaligned, facing the air immediately over its spine.

In a lightless night a big tom's screech, a fox drowned or about to be drowned in a sinkhole, Little Charlie's ghost laughingly traversing a slush-covered fairway.

He took in a breath and, holding it, leaned into the bin; its narrow dimensions allowed him, where he was at, to reach into all of it. He looked under each trash bag; he searched in the bin's every corner; he found no half-full duffel bag; he found no duffel bags at all, no clothes, no gun.

* * *

In the station's men's room he washed and dried his hands and face. He entered the store. Florence stood before a big wall cooler, staring into it. "I don't want more beer," she said. "Do you?"

"No."

"How 'bout a Coke. A Coke and some Twinkies. You ought to eat something or you'll faint dead away."

"I ain't hungry still."

Florence took a sixteen-ounce Coke from the cooler and from a rack next to it two twin-packs of Twinkies. She touched a finger to her and Rankin's reflections in the cooler's glass door. "It's odd to be standing here looking at yourself and to be in another place watching yourself doing it."

"Who you talking about?"

"The one of us who's flying."

"What other place you mean?"

"I don't know. It's a nice place though."

"I didn't find in that dumpster any of what I should of."

"You looked at least." She made it sound as if that was a good thing, as if the God she claimed to know so well would think so too. Rankin took from her the Coke and Twinkies. He carried them to the front and paid for them. He passed to Florence the bag the cashier handed him. They walked back outside and got in the Tranny.

"A garbage truck, Samson, like as not came and emptied it earlier today."

Rankin started the engine. He put the car in drive; he headed it toward the road.

* * *

Darkness like black paint in a drawing of night perforated by a monster's illumined eyes; a deer flashing before the headlights; coolish air, a pine scent, the tires whine rushing in through Florence's cracked window, her tossed cigarette butt a dying ember in the gloom. A visible shiver in her delicate bones. A lighted object appearing too big for the road suddenly coming at them like a suppressed nightmare (*A crew of A-block Thugs on his second day inside ambushing Charlie*

Rankin in the shower, twelve of them taking turns fucking him up the ass, the ones awaiting their go at him keeping him pinned to the floor, Rankin never crying out, speaking, even moaning so that but for his breathing and his wide open eyes watching his blood swirling in the drain he could've been dead) the object passing them, revealed to be only a truck, smaller than it had seemed; words from Florence.

Rankin glanced her way.

"Him again," she said, as if in response to a conversation he'd initiated.

Rankin replied only by staring at her.

She rolled up her window, patted herself down searching for a fresh smoke, pulled one finally out of her left sleeve, said, "Charlie Rankin."

"Why you bringing him up?"

"I didn't. You did."

"What're you talking about?"

"As that tractor trailer was going by you said his name."

"Why would I do that?"

"I'm wondering, Samson."

Rankin, looking back out the windshield, ran a hand over his eyes, smearing in his vision the world captured in the Tranny's headlights, creating in his mind a picture of him and this girl he'd dared picture himself in the future with as jumbled thoughts in the flickering recesses of a hallucinating brain. He heard himself say, "It was Buddha got him to start talking again after four days."

"Charlie Rankin?"

"Right."

In response to being touched on his shoulder, looking up from where he was eating alone in a corner of the cafeteria (still too sore to walk or shit right) for the first time encountering the hypnotic eyes of William Pettigrew.

"Why'd he stop talking?"

Rankin blinked. "He sometimes—ever since he was a kid—just goes mute, nothing'd come out of his mouth for dying. Afterward he don't remember much, 'cept maybe in his dreams, of what it was shut him up."

"How'd this Buddha get him talking again."

"He invited him to play checkers."

"Checkers?"

"Charlie Rankin loves checkers. He'd only ever played them against himself though because no one, not even when he was a kid, had ever asked him to play before. They started playing regular in Buddha's cell. Buddha told Charlie Rankin rabid animals die slow and painful from their own madness if they aren't put out of their misery. The day after he said it two of 'em who'd attacked Charlie Rankin were dead, two others fucked up for life in the infirmary, the rest begging for solitary."

"Buddha sounds like a powerful guy."

"You don't want to cross him. He's got a long arm."

"The little deskman at the Sinclair one a the fingers at the end of his arm?"

Rankin nodded. "Charlie Rankin too. And me. We're riding in a car paid for with his money. You're wearing clothes bought by him."

"I'd as soon take 'em off, put back on my old ones."

"It's too late for that."

"What do you mean?"

"His memory, says Buddha, goes back as far as time. He don't forget a thing, 'specially what's owed him."

* * *

The Tranny's highbeams delineated in the darkness a guy with his thumb out, holding a briefcase; he stood on the roadside in a knee-length raincoat and an odd sort of hat bunched atop his head; Rankin applied the brakes.

He stopped the Tranny next to the guy. Florence opened her door, called out, "We're heading, it looks like, to the next town. That help ya?"

The guy wordlessly approached them. Florence, moving her seat back forward, scrunched herself against the dash; the guy climbed into the rearseat. He smelled of aftershave; the sides of his head were razored; he had a bulbous nose; the cloth pile on his hat was comprised of earflaps and a chin strap. His at once blank and penetrating stare unnerved Rankin. Rankin started driving again. Florence said, "My smoking bother you?"

The guy didn't answer. He seemed to be studying the back of Florence's head, then Rankin's face as Rankin eyed what he could see of him in the rearview mirror. Florence turned to the backseat. "I'll open a window it does."

The guy gazed blankly forward.

"You from around here?" asked Florence.

The guy didn't say.

"Where you headed to?"

No answer.

Florence looked at Rankin. "I think he's deaf or something."

"And he's a mute too," said Rankin.

"How do you know?"

Rankin wasn't sure how he knew, only that he did know. He glanced again at the guy; the guy appeared as only a dark shadow behind him. Rankin pictured the guy having been there, over his right shoulder, since Rankin had gotten out of prison. Florence said, "Turn on the dome light."

Rankin looked at her.

"Maybe he can read lips," Florence told him. "If he can't, we can talk to him with our hands."

"I don't want to talk to him."

"That's not sociable, Samson. Why'd you give him a ride, you don't want to talk to him?"

"I don't know why I gave him a ride. I only know I ain't going to talk to him." Rankin heard what he took for the guy's brief-case snapping open, the guy's hands fumbling around inside the case. A white glow appeared ahead of them. Rankin remembered a donut shop sign with two burned out letters in it, feeling as if he were the main character in a movie about an assassin, making a phone call and hanging up when someone answered. "I'm going to at least try to talk to him," said Florence; she pushed on the dome light. "I don't want him to think we're rude."

She turned to the back seat, as they came out of the dark-ness (Rankin had the sensation pole lights had been eyeing them from above all along and just now had revealed them-selves) onto a boulevard alive with businesses and fast food joints. Rankin turned up the radio. In the corner of his eye Florence was making exaggerated hand motions, silent mouth movements. He heard what sounded like papers rustling in the backseat. He avoided looking in the rearview mirror. A road sign declared "Welcome to Willimette." The knowledge came home to him that to get out from under Buddha's weight he'd have to live, or relive, a nightmare.

He thought, somewhere soon he'd need to get a gun.

He wondered if Florence had a clue of the danger she was in poking at the part of him she sensed but hadn't seen.

A frost bump under the tires sent a shiver through the car. Visible past the streetlamps downcast arc were stars, an air-plane's pulsating light, a winged shape bisecting the blackness.

"He wants out," said Florence.

Rankin looked at her.

"Up here he does." She chinpointed ahead to her side, at a little cluster of buildings—a gas station, a restaurant, a Krispy Kreme shop emblazoned by a neon sign in which both Rs were dead. Rankin swung the car into a parking lot facing the build-ings; he stopped it before an outdoor phone; averting his eyes from the Tranny's interior, he aimed them out his window; he felt, at the same time he was anticipating it, a tap on his shoulder; a tremor passed through him; his stomach pain intensified as it had in that church; Florence said, "He's trying to give you something, Samson."

Rankin turned to the backseat; the ear and chin flaps now dangling loosely around his face, the hitchhiker held a pamphlet out toward Rankin.

"It's got a picture on its front of a guy burning in hell," said Florence.

Rankin suddenly had an overwhelming fear of being recognized. "Who's the guy in hell look like?"

"He doesn't look like anybody alive. He's covered with boils and stuff."

Rankin said, "Tell Elmer Fudd the ride's over."

"You'll make him feel good you take one of his books, Samson."

"He don't stop looking at me like he knows me I'll make him dead."

"I think he's retarded," said Florence, "and this is just something for him to do." She smiled at the guy, directing at him a bunch of hand motions.

The guy, eyeing Rankin still, pointed to the roof.

"What's he saying?" demanded Rankin, imagining the guy was seeing him not just sitting there, but at places in the past and at a place, after this night was over, down the road.

"He was answering a question I asked him."

"What question?"

"Who does he work for."

Rankin whipped from his wallet and handed Florence a hundred dollar bill. "Give him this and tell him to get out."

The guy acted blind to the money. He shut his briefcase (the sharp snap it made struck Rankin as the closest thing to a voice from the mute). Touching her sweater over her heart, Florence, extending in her other hand the hundred toward the guy, mouthed to him, "Accept it for the pleasure of your company."

The guy made no motion either to take the cash or to leave; he kept looking at Rankin. "Use it for the Lord's work." Florence formed the words deliberately into the mute's face.

Rankin reached over and snatched the C-note from her; he pulled another one out of his wallet, grabbed the guy's coat front, then pushed both bills down into the coat's outer left pocket. He told the mute, "You don't know me, get it? You ain't never seen me before. You ain't never going to see, think or dream about me again."

The mute grinned at him.

Rankin leaned into the back seat, opened the left rear door, and shoved the guy out of the car into the parking lot. He slammed shut the door. He sped the car forward. He stopped it at the entrance to the road.

Florence said, "Was it last night he saw you last, Samson?"

Rankin revved the Tranny's engine, not answering her.

"Was it in this same parking lot?"

"You got it all wrong," said Rankin.

"What do I?"

"About what's going to happen on this ride you wanted to take with me."

"I ain't got a crystal ball, Samson. I don't see the future. I only see you so twisted up inside you can't eat and me here taking a chance on you."

"I don't aim to die. I aim to live long's I can."

"That's good. You're back to wanting to the way most everybody else does."

Rankin looked at her.

"Last I heard you was ready to cash in your chips, try a new game."

"What I got to do to live ain't what most everybody else has got to do to live."

"You talking about you being a finger at the end of this guy Buddha's arm?"

"You don't take his money and walk away."

"Is that what you did?"

Rankin, without replying, put the Tranny in reverse and backed it up so fast its tires squealed on the asphalt. He halted it next to the phone. Leaving the car running in park, he hopped out of it. Florence shouted to him something he didn't catch.

No phone book hung next to the phone, only a thin chain dangling from an empty hook.

Rankin glanced over his shoulder at the restaurant; facing him in its doorway stood the deaf-mute holding an armful of his pamphlets. Rankin turned away from him; he picked up the phone's receiver, withdrew a quarter from his pants pocket, dropped the quarter in the change slot, and dialed the first seven numbers that came to him. On the line's other end a phone began to ring. It rang four times, then was picked up. "Hello?" a man's voice inquired.

"Who is this?" asked Rankin.

"Who is it that's asking?"

"I'm taking a survey and need your name for it."

"I don't give out my name to strangers," said the voice. The phone went dead.

* * *

The thought struck him that miles ago he ought to have dumped Florence, that if he didn't dump her soon he was as good as signing either his own or her death warrant.

They passed two bus stops and a taxi stand where he could have left her with a bunch of the money, told her to find her own way home, and lied to her he'd catch up with her later. But when he imagined driving away from her, watching her disappear to him in his rearview mirror, he imagined the last good part of him disappearing with her. He envisioned her still with him some-place way past all this, someplace that would feel as good to the two of them together as those woods he'd run off into as a kid had felt to him alone. "What's his or her name?" she asked.

Rankin looked at her, the motions of her near-constant smoking appearing to him to be as unconscious as breathing. She treated his silence as a question.

"Whoever you're on your way to see. Isn't that what this ride—and your bellyache—is about?"

That she'd not asked him earlier where they were headed or why they were going there he'd taken as evidence that maybe she really was an angel, a sorceress, something not entirely of this world. Now he wondered if she was just stupid; he had an impulse to tell her that knowing him as much as she seemed to want to know him could get her dead in a heartbeat. Instead he said, "What'd your old boyfriend do for cash?"

She blew smoke out her nostrils. "Most recently he worked in a video store."

"Renting 'em out, you mean?"

"And rewinding them when customers didn't, putting them back on the shelves. Once in a while somebody would ask him for a recommendation and he'd be in hog Heaven thinking he was Roger Ebert."

"What ones did he like?"

"Horror ones." She scrunched up her face, showing Rankin her opinion of horror movies. "I never told him about LuAnn's films."

"Why didn't you?"

"He wouldn't been able to see nobody but me in 'em. Not like how you and I can, Samson."

As if recalling scenes from a movie he'd watched half-asleep Rankin had flashbacks of getting lost in a stolen car on these or similar streets. "I like you," he said.

She nodded. "I knew it without you saying it."

They entered a renovated riverfront area called Old Town. "I never have much a woman—or anybody—before."

Florence pulled from her lips the cigarette, tapped ash from it into her empty Coke can. "Yeah, so—tell me something I don't know."

Rankin tried to get in touch with what he'd been thinking, the feelings he'd been experiencing, when last he'd been on this route. He couldn't though. He remembered only looking into a mirror over his visor and seeing a stone-killer's face. "Charlie Rankin," he said.

Florence returned the cigarette to her mouth. "Charlie Rankin. What about Charlie Rankin?"

"You wanted me to tell you something you don't know." Rankin, by rote, moved into the right hand lane, passing shops and restaurants, close to half of them unlighted, and pedestrians, going in and out of them, weaving along a boardwalk lined with yellow street lamps. In the distance, past the milieu, pinpoints of light marked a bridge spanning the river. "You don't know him."

He stopped behind a column of traffic at a red light. Florence leaned back against her door, facing him. "What about him should I know?"

Rankin eased open his window; into the car came a whiff of buttered popcorn, exhaust fumes, snatches of conversation, string music from a band of old duffers playing under a gazebo near the water to a sparse crowd, a foghorn's muted bay. "He's Buddha's biggest convert. He weren't nothing till Buddha made him what he is." Rankin stared hard at Florence. Florence stared hard back at him, smoking without her hands. "Buddha gives him a job, he's going to do it."

A longhaired kid on a bike darted through the two feet of space between the Tranny's front bumper and the car before it, headed for the boardwalk. The light changed to green. The vehicles preceding them didn't move. Florence said, "You ought to take a blow from the place you're at." She made a wavy line in the air with one hand. "Come cool out with me on this beach awhile."

"You ain't on no beach. You're riding right Goddamn next to me."

"What makes you right and me wrong?"

"I know where I am at least." A couple of horns honked. Voices from behind them shouted. Rankin envisioned the Charlie Rankin that William Pettigrew had given a face to coming alive in the skin of Charlie Rankin driving the Tranny. "And you'd do best not forgetting you ain't anywhere but here too."

Florence wordlessly snuffed out in the ashtray her cigarette; she didn't light another one.

"I'll leave you off, pick you up on the way back."

"On the way back from where?"

"I got business the other side that bridge ahead."

Florence rolled down her window. "Magic Carpet Ride" reached them from a neighboring truck's radio. "If you tell me to get out now I will," said Florence, "but don't look to find me later. You won't have this girl better-looking than any girl you've ever seen still thinking good thoughts about you."

"I'm trying to tell you."

"What are you trying to tell me?"

"You can't, Goddammit, be as stupid as how you come off."

"Damn straight I can't be. And you'd be smart to bear in mind I ain't."

A siren started whining; a red bubble light was seen flashing on its way toward them. A sudden fear of being swooped down upon and ripped to pieces prompted Rankin to reach out and snatch Florence's purse from her. She didn't try to stop him from taking it. He withdrew from it her .22, checked to see it was loaded still. In the same tone she'd invited Rankin to join her on some beach she wasn't at, Florence said, "How could they—the cops—ever know to look for you in this car?"

"What?"

"Unless somebody told them to and that person would have

to know both that you were in the car and that you'd done something the cops might want to talk to you about."

Rankin's sudden paranoia focused on the wall phone outside the room in Randy's Watering Hole he'd found Florence in with Stitch Marks. As if reading his mind, Florence, nodding at the .22, said, "Was me who first offered it to you, remember?"

Rankin, not answering her, slipped the .22 into his pants waist beneath his shirt; he had the sensation that Florence, even while sitting next to him, was in his head, turning over— maybe even orchestrating—his thoughts. He peered through the windshield to see if the flashing light was still coming for them, but the vehicle carrying the light (Rankin could now make it out as a cop car) had stopped a hundred feet up the road, beneath the traffic light. Florence stuck her head out her window.

"Something's down," she said, her voice sounding to Rankin as if it were coming out of a hole in the earth. She pulled her head back inside. "I can't see who or what, just a crowd around it in the intersection."

Charlie Rankin ignoring a warning from the wide-open eyes of a warm body lying dead from no apparent reason in the road before him.

Rankin heard himself say, "Two people maybe died last night that shouldn't have."

"What people?"

"They lived in the wrong house."

"Are you sure?"

"What?"

"Which house did they live in?"

Rankin didn't answer her.

"Trust me, Samson. I'm in a soul older and wiser than yours."

Rankin looked at her.

Florence placed a hand on his chest; as if her touch were

regulating it, his heart, as she felt of it, accelerated. "It acts to want to break out of you."

Rankin pushed her hand away. "I told you to get out, didn't I?"

"No. You didn't. Are you telling me to now?"

Against his intention to nod Rankin shook his head. "What are you doing to me? I can't think right."

"You're thinking good enough to drive." The Tranny, under Rankin's direction, was following the now advancing line of traffic. "I'm awful proud of you."

"What?"

"You better stop for this cop though. We wouldn't want him to ask to see your license."

His hand up at them the cop stood directly under the traffic light; off to his right were two more cops, a pickup with a stove-in front, a sanitation truck into the back of which three men in jumpsuits were hoisting a brown-and-white animal cadaver, the size of a German shepherd dog, that Rankin was convinced he'd seen, dead or acting dead, on another road.

"Poor thing," said Florence.

Rankin, fighting an urge to get out of the car and surrender to the cop for every crime he'd ever committed or dreamed he'd committed, swabbed at his face from which sweat was boiling.

The cop waved them forward.

Rankin eased the Tranny ahead, through the intersection, not looking left or right.

* * *

On the far side of the bridge, Florence, as if she'd been on the lookout for it, pointed him into a grass pulloff shrouded by evergreens. "No peeking," she said.

Dangling her big shoulder bag, she stepped from the car, walked to the left edge of the headlights arc, raised her sweater over her waist, lowered her underpants, squatted, and peed.

She rearranged her clothes, and moved deeper into the trees; in the near-dark Rankin could make out only her shape; she appeared to him to be taking off her head, putting on another one. She approached his window, tapped on it until he rolled it down, told him, "See if I don't rev you up more this way."

Shoulder-length dirty-blonde hair falling from the face of that strangled woman gazing up dead-eyed at Little Charlie.

The woman's upper body came through the window, into the car. Rankin jumped back from it. In the dashboard light's faint glow, the face hunting his had a bloodless pallor.

The woman pulled her head out of the car, went around to and opened the passenger door; placing her bag on the seat, she climbed in next to it, then shut the door. She touched a finger to her long, flowing hair. "Ever since I had mine chopped off a week ago I carry this with me case the mood hits me to be again the woman I was."

Rankin shrunk from her.

She reached out and pressed to his forehead a hand as cold as frozen earth. "My God. You're burning up."

"I feel sick."

"I should have seen it coming."

Sweat stinging and blurring his eyes, Rankin tried to identify the woman as Florence.

She unbuttoned his shirt, slipped it off of him, Rankin (his hand, his whole body trembling) feeling powerless to stop her. She shut down the car. The interior light disappeared. She unbuckled his pants. She whispered, "I can feel in your skin the beautiful baby you were."

Sounding to himself as weak and faraway as Florence had talking to him with her head out the window in Old Town, Rankin said, "You poisoned me."

"How could I have? You ain't ate nor drank nothing I offered you."

"You did it to me another way then."

"You did it to yourself from the trouble churning in you."

"I'm dizzy. One thing seems like another and everything together seems like nothing."

"Hold my cold body you'll maybe cool down."

"You know what's good for you you'll stay off me."

"I never know what's good for me till I do it."

"I keep trying to warn you."

"About what?"

"Who I am."

"I know who you are." The voice came now from the car's opposite side; hands no longer were touching him. "You had a dog you loved more than anything in the world that died and you're hoping, after you die, for a thing called reincarnation."

Little Charlie's mother whispering to Little Charlie, entwined in her arms, that if being loved for being beautiful was a sin both him and her were doomed to eternal hell.

"I'm Charlie Rankin."

"I'm Florence Merriweather Jane."

Rankin saw in the dark void right of him the orange glow at the end of a burning cigarette, heard lips snap sucking on it, bare skin squeaking on the vinyl seat cover, lungs emptying; he sensed, then smelled, smoke enveloping him. He said, "You're in it now—I can't let you out of it—because now you know, don't you?"

"Know what?"

"Why I'm here."

"Why don't you tell me why you think you're here."

"I owe Buddha my life."

"That doesn't answer why you're here."

"I musta fucked up killing who he paid me to last night, so I'm back to do it for sure tonight. Then we can eat, go to any restaurant you want."

"You think you came here tonight to kill someone?"

Rivulets of sweat descending his belly into his groin felt to Rankin like small insects. "I know why I'm here. I don't know why you are."

"Who do you think you came here to kill?"

"Some guy"—(*Cartilage and bone filled flesh snapping as Little Charlie squeezed it; a human face draining of blood above Little Charlie's grasp*)—"it don't matter who."

"It will to him if you do it. It will to you too. It'll make you sicker and sicker."

Pursuant to a sudden panicky feeling Rankin reached down for the gun in his belt; he found it gone, his pants, his underwear off. While burning up, he was shivering.

"Where's the .22?"

"Likely with your jeans, on the floor where you shucked them."

"I don't remember."

Out of the dark came a hand holding a tissue; it dabbed at the perspiration wetting his cheeks. "It acts, Charlie Rankin, to want to pour out of you."

Rankin reached out and seized her by a shoulder. "Who are you?"

"Who is it you keep mistaking me for?"

"Where'd you get that hair?"

"At the Alto Wig Emporium."

Rankin snatched off the wig. He threw it into the back seat. He put his hands to her throat, half-intending to wrap them around it, but they fell lower, onto her back, and he found himself squeezing or hugging her. Florence moved so that she was directly facing him. She lay down on the seat beneath him (her sweater was up around her neck and she was naked beneath it) then pulled him down onto her, her deathly cold body as welcome to his feverish one as an unexpected breeze on a sweltering day. "Get inside me and feel better," she said, putting him between her legs.

"Now make love to me."

Even with all her help—and as much as he wanted to—he couldn't. He slipped mostly out of her, then fell into unconsciousness.

* * *

In that danger-charged darkness he shared with her and whoever Little Charlie night after night dreaming he was a clerk (selling exercise equipment or groceries or cooking utensils or movie tickets or throws with fifty-dollar whores and their sons) smiling pleasantly to his customers, while picking out one of them each day to follow home, murder, hack into bits, and incinerate.

Feeling only slightly heated, he woke with his head in Florence's lap.

He wondered if he'd had a fever at all, if she'd only convinced him of it.

He gazed up at her face (her eyes were closed, her lips slackly together as if that were their natural position) seeing in it, without comprehending what he was seeing (he was aware only that he was feeling sadness and anger), every beautiful thing, sight, person beyond his reach.

He sat up, turned to and twisted down his window.

The entering air made steam rise from his wet skin, sent through him an eruption greater than a shiver.

Who? Who? Who? inquired an owl in the trees left of him.

Over the blackened river past the windshield a fog bank stalked them, into the dark sky beyond it a faint white halo from the lights of old town intruding. Jolted anew by stomach pain (his pain seemed to him now to have plagued him forever) Rankin abruptly realized he'd been sick as long as he could remember, that what he was suffering from had been festering in him since birth. "You slept two and a half hours," said Florence.

Rankin stayed staring out the window.

"I guess you feel better," she said.

"I had a bout of something. Maybe 'cause I didn't eat."

"Are you hungry now?"

"You know I ain't."

Florence pulled on her underpants. "I love you no matter. That other—fucking, what all—it's just mechanics."

Rankin, still not looking at her, reached down and picked up his clothes and the .22 from under the steering wheel.

"You could learn how to love nice."

"You don't know what you're talking about."

"I could teach you."

Rankin yanked on his jeans, buckled them, then got into his shirt. He buttoned it. Then he put on his boots. He said, "My mother made a good omelet."

"Omelet?"

"As good as I've ever eaten."

"What sort of one did she make, Charlie?"

"Whatever was left from what we'd ate for a couple days before she'd put in one—potatoes, hamburg, bacon, macaroni, little broken up chunks of rolls." Rankin slipped the .22 into his pantswaist. He faced his window again. "I ever forget how good them omelets was and how she'd make one just for me, 'cause didn't nobody else but me like 'em, I'd as soon die the same second."

Florence straightened her sweater, her dark reflection in Rankin's window half-blotting out to him his own image. "If you could forget, Charlie, you wouldn't be Samson."

"I can't make nothing out of half what you say."

Florence didn't answer him.

Rankin turned to her, seeing less of her straight on than he'd seen of her in her reflection; he had a vision of her red, curdled nipples, as she'd laid beneath him earlier, protruding from her breasts like the heads of two bodies in quicksand; at the same time he saw in his mind a mailbox, marked #210 Viner Lane. "There's a 7-11 up the road. You promise not to call the cops I'll leave you at it. You can catch a ride home from there."

"It's up to you, Charlie. It always has been."

"You think it ain't going to happen if you're along, like me not taking you out to dinner after I said I would?"

"I told you, Charlie—you want to never see me again just say it."

"You aren't ready for the things you think you're ready for—because what you know about them is just talk."

"About what?"

"Charlie Rankin."

Florence lit a cigarette. "I think, Charlie, I know more about why you're here than you do."

Rankin suddenly had the sensation that a part of his mind had been usurped from him and implanted with a picture of a woman in shadows, suffocating; in the same moment, the fog bank that had been nearing the Tranny enveloped it, extinguishing the sky's meager light, eclipsing Florence to him. Rankin could see only the burning end of her cigarette. "I'm guessing when my soul was as young as yours is now, Charlie, I musta been as full of anger and violence as you."

The faceless woman in Rankin's mind reached her hands out to him.

The cigarette end, bobbing, brightened and crackled across from him. "And spent a fucked-up lifetime from it."

A gentle gust rocked the Tranny.

"But here I am on the far side of it, Charlie—feeling only love for the good in you only an old soul who's been where you're at can see."

The woman disappeared. Rankin said, "You're whacked out. Or a witch or something."

Florence cackled (not a funny or an amused cackle). "Who do you think died for being in that wrong house last night, Charlie?"

Rankin, not answering her, started the car; instead of penetrating the fog, the headlights turned back onto the Tranny a radiant, non-illuminating denseness. Florence opened her window. She tossed out her cigarette. She picked up the wig from the floor; holding it out toward him, she nodded at it. "Good to know, I guess"—she stuffed the wig in her purse—"you like the new me better than the old me."

Rankin grabbed her by an arm. "What all words come out of me back then?"

"Say again, Charlie."

"When I was out my head them few minutes."

"Out of whose head when?"

Rankin dropped her arm and put the car in gear. "After that 7-11 there ain't no more stops—not for this car—'cept the last one."

"I don't need to go to it, Charlie—the 7-11. Unless you need me to."

"We take a right up here at an intersection, then a left. It ain't more than fifteen minutes from here to the end, understand?"

"You're driving, Charlie."

Rankin, his mind's eye suddenly seeing the route he would follow as clearly as if it appeared on the windshield before him, angled the Tranny out onto the road.

* * *

Little Charlie over and over again reading bad shit in the sons of bitches eyes, voices, scents, postures (they were so transparent and his mother blind as a bat) and over and over again being as helpless against the shit as he was to escape being Little Charlie.

"The guy's name is Maynard Cass."

Silence from Florence.

"He lives at 210 Viner Lane."

Nothing.

"The places are spread way out, so this time no fucking around—no mask, no bushwhacking, no peeking in fucking windows."

As if he were talking to himself.

"I douse the headlights, pull her into the drive a few yards, shut her down so she can't be seen from the road or house, then walk up, knock on the door like a guy from a breakdown needing a phone—that's it."

Too late, he thought, she's come down from her high and opened her eyes for the first time on Charlie Rankin; too late she's wishing she was back doing blow with her old boyfriend, the video store guy; too late she's knowing that she should have left Charlie Rankin at the 7-11, that she should have never taken up with him at all.

"Past them trees lays a golf course." He waved at the window beyond Florence. It seemed to him that in the same moment his destination had become clear to him he was at it. "It's all rich people live on it. Probably get their windows broke all the time by golf balls and just buy new ones like most people do a cup of coffee."

Not a word back to him.

"I know what the guy looks like"—a picture of the guy in a photograph had, that second, popped into his head—"so if it's him answers I'll put one in him right off, then finish him with a head shot. If it ain't, I'll make who does bring me to him and do him wherever I find him, tie up the other one, and go."

"Chill, Charlie," said Florence, her voice sounding no different than it had when she'd been telling about her cat that died.

Rankin stared toward her.

"You ain't got to be scared."

She didn't sound at all scared.

"Scared?" Rankin remembered her with that wig on, how it

had seemed to transform and age her. "What do you mean scared? I was born to do this. I ain't scared."

"Just follow your instincts, Charlie."

"What?"

"They'll take you to the right place."

The oddly hopeful thought struck Rankin that he was still on this road at the beginning of the night before, that anything past then hadn't happened—or hadn't happened yet—except in one of Little Charlie's dreams. A sign ahead for the River Run Golf Course Club House reacquainted him with an angry, unjust feeling that had him picturing Charlie Rankin, shivering in a hail storm, peeking through a window into a room warmed by a fireplace at a bunch of golf course guys (one golf course guy looked in his vision of golf course guys like every other golf course guy) drinking, talking, laughing, living high off the world's short supply of pure oxygen, leaving the Charlie Rankins outside that room only sick, polluted air to breathe.

"Do you want me to come with you?"

"What?"

"Once we get there—to the house—should I come up to the door with you? Would that make it easier?"

Trying to distinguish Florence's face in the semi-dark, Rankin saw in his mind again that woman in shadows; he couldn't tell if in reaching out to him the woman was begging for mercy, asking for help or pointing Rankin out accusingly to someone not in Rankin's vision. He blinked at Florence, tried to bring her into focus. "What I want is you to stay in the Goddamn car."

"You change your mind let me know."

"Why would I change my mind?"

"Mine usually gives me plenty of reasons to change it from doing one thing to doing another thing right up until I do the thing I end up doing."

"Are you so fucked-up you don't get what's about to go down here?"

"I feel about as clear-headed as I ever get, Charlie. How 'bout you? How you feel?"

"Like you're talking at me from a thousand Goddamn different directions outta that many heads. That's how."

He wondered what she'd done to his mind to make him not dump her one of the hundreds of times he should have dumped her; then, with a sudden tyrannized feeling, he wondered what he'd do to her after he'd finished doing what he'd come here to do because Charlie Rankin wasn't one to leave loose ends. "206, Charlie."

Stark white in the dashboard's luminescence her hand, in the space between them, motioned at a mailbox at the base of a driveway out his window.

Rankin slowed the Tranny.

On the hill above the mailbox appeared an unlighted conical-shaped building shades blacker than the night. "How many more before the one, Charlie?" inquired Florence, as if Rankin hadn't just told her the address.

"One more," he said, "on this side. Then the place."

"You sure?" she asked, as if she thought he might not be, as if she was half-certain he'd miscalculated.

"Goddammit—yes. 210."

"210. That's the one?"

"Ain't that what I said? 210—it's what was written on the Goddamn piece of paper with the guy's picture!"

"I don't doubt the guy lives there, Charlie. At 210."

"What the hell you asking me?"

Florence, instead of answering him, lightly touched his arm. She pointed ahead, to the next driveway; the mailbox (if there was one) marking the drive was obscured to them; a fluorescent pole lamp partly lit the way up to a rectangular-shaped house showing only two exterior lights.

Passing the place, they started into a long bend. Rankin decelerated the car to a virtual crawl.

Florence said, "A quiet, peaceful neighborhood."

Rankin thought, how could it be (quiet, peaceful) after last night? Unless last night was still in the future. Unless to this point last night had taken place only in a dream in which he was in the aftermath of.

"Or like nobody lives in it at all," whispered Florence.

Rankin, struck by an eerie sensation, glanced in the rearview mirror. As he had since they'd entered the area, he saw only darkness behind and in front of them. A few scattered lights in the trees were the only indications of a human presence in the neighborhood; since entering it, they'd encountered no pedestrians or vehicles; even the clubhouse had been dark. Rankin had a vision of empty homes, their occupants out in the woods, eyeing the Tranny as it passed them.

Dragging its hindquarters, bleeding from one hip, a yellow dog crossed the road in front of them. The animal bared its teeth at the car. Florence either gasped or loudly drew air in around her cigarette. Rankin rolled down his window. From the early winter night no scent reached him, no hint of life. He closed the window. They rounded the corner. A thin mist that had been moving with them, left them. The Tranny's headlight beams suddenly seemed boundless in the forward blackness. Rankin switched them off. At the same time that he remembered counting to himself "210" as he'd driven by it the night before, he saw atop a rise past his window the indistinct outline of a large building hidden in trees. A single light shone in either end of the structure. Rankin turned the Tranny into a snaking, unlighted drive leading to it. He stopped the car twenty feet from the road. He shut it down. He rolled his head at Florence.

"This is the one, Charlie," she said, "you're positive?"

Rankin, not responding to her, got out the .22, withdrew its clip, checked to make sure it was full. "Some things ain't worth giving up for nothing, Charlie." Rankin returned the clip to the gun and the gun into his pantswaist. "Like hunger—for food, for fucking, for laughter, for love—I'd be happier locked up for life feeling them things and not being able to satisfy 'em than walking the world never feeling 'em again."

Rankin reached out and pulled the cigarette from her mouth.

"They ain't got the death penalty in this state, Charlie. I read that in the newspaper."

In the sky's faint light entering through her window Florence's head seemed to Rankin to elongate, as if two invisible hands gripping her at the nose were pulling in opposite directions, and her mouth to expand as if she were working up to swallowing Charlie Rankin whole. "Who you talking to?"

"I'm talking to Samson, Charlie Rankin."

Rankin extinguished her cigarette in the ashtray between them. "Likely all your smoke's what's been making me sick."

He took his gravity knife from his jeans pocket and flicked out its blade. "Don't be scared," he said.

"Don't you be, Charlie."

Rankin took hold of her seat belt and cut it out of its retainers. Then he did the same to his own. "Birds fall from the sky don't nobody notice."

"He notices, Charlie."

"The man in the moon—that who you mean?"

"Out there walking, Charlie"—Florence flicked her eyes at the night—"listen, okay? Everything'll come out right you trust what you hear."

"I'm maybe going to dream it."

"Don't dream it, Charlie. Dreams don't matter. This matters."

"Put your hands behind you."

Florence, turning to the door, allowed Rankin, with one of the straps to tie her hands together at the base of her back. "Was me who wanted to come with you, Charlie, and you who wanted to bring me, remember? Why would I leave you now?"

Rankin bound her ankles together with the second strap, then took the keys out of the ignition and the flashlight from the glove compartment. He put them both in his jacket pocket, got out of the car, locked its two doors, and headed up the driveway toward the house.

* * *

The soft, rhythmic tattoo of his boots hitting the pavement; a rustling from a scant wind moving the shrubbery left and right of him; a whiff of hemlock; glimpses of his breath hitting the rimy air; a clammy feel in his sweat-damp clothes.

Two hundred feet before the house the drive split, forming what looked to be a big circle in the frontyard, Rankin picturing Maynard Cass and all his golf club friends, in their golf club type cars, never in that O-shaped drive having to back up, turn around, look behind them, see again what they'd run over on the way in and forgotten about.

The overcast sky above the house a dark room's fogged-up window with, here and there, eyes pressed to it.

Chester Rhimes yelling from the bed he shared with Little Charlie's mother to Little Charlie trying to sleep invisibly on the room's couch "don't think I can't see you over there in the dark hating me."

A building half the size of the house but bigger than any place Rankin had lived at stood three-quarters of the way along the loop's upper course, behind a metal fence. From the building's rear corner, attached to its roof line, a single halogen bulb shone onto a plastic-covered, egg-shaped swimming pool. A tennis court lay in dark shadows past the pool.

Buddha, tousling Rankin's hair, telling him tennis was a gentleman's sport, not a sport for Charlie Rankin, then, as Rankin rubbed his back for him, how he—William Pettigrew—had won some club tennis championship three years running.

Rankin, on his way to Maynard Cass's big house, gripped and swung an imaginary racquet; he tried to envision himself loping gazelle-like after a little bouncing ball. The image wouldn't take. He flung his fake racquet into the foliage, a voice in his head screaming, "any son of a bitch's bad luck they look straight on tonight at Charlie Rankin!"

A rustling more focused than the wind could cause came from his right flank.

He remembered Florence nodding at the night, telling him to listen in it. The thought struck him that if he returned to the car at that moment she'd be gone from it, that he'd been foolish to think he could keep her in a place he wanted her at, that even killing her he couldn't keep her out of his head, that she'd maybe never been alive to begin with. He remembered her in that long blonde hair and the blonde woman in shadows in his mind reaching out to him. The rustling, just ahead of him now, grew in intensity.

Pitch-black night upon pitch-black night in which Little Charlie's senses were never at rest (not even in his dreams) when a word, a footstep, an exhale might ignite an explosion.

Rankin drew the .22.

Ten feet forward of him a four-legged shape broke from the bushes; it stopped in the drive, facing him. The night-obscured creature (it resembled a wolf or large dog) made no noise or movement. Rankin got the flashlight from his pocket. Training the .22 on the animal, he hit it with the light's beam.

Part boxer, he surmised of the cur in his path, part bloodhound, part whatever, the whole of it shit-kicked, the same mutt that had crossed the road snarling at the Tranny earlier.

The look of its injured hip suggested it had been bitten or stabbed. Blood and filth matted its yellow fur. The septum dangled from its nose, as if it had been half-ripped out. Porcupine quills protruded from its snout. From weakness or rage (Rankin couldn't tell which) it was quivering slightly. He imagined it, while staring blandly into the light toward him, contemplating whether to lunge for Rankin's throat or to lie down and mewl before him. Rankin couldn't decide if to loathe or pity such a creature.

He pushed the gun into his belt. He stepped slowly toward the dog. The animal warily raised its ears, not otherwise reacting to him. A rawhide collar adorned its neck. Rankin knelt down beside the animal. It smelled of the awful times its appearance screamed to the world it was infected with, radiated from its pelt anger-and-petrified-induced heat, breathed raggedly through its mouth. Rankin envisioned Mister Full Boat the day after Rankin had gone inside, gazing up at Sam Jenkins, suddenly finding its life in that son of a bitch's hands.

He reached down to the dog's neck. He slipped his fingers behind its collar. The cur made a warning growl. Ignoring it, Rankin angled the light at its collar; words were carved into it. Rankin inclined at and read from the circlet, "I never warmed to this dog, though it gave me no reason to shoot it, so I've cut it loose in the hope whoever finds it will take more of a liking to it than I did."

Rankin lay the light on the drive, aiming it at the animal. He fitted the bend of his left elbow around its neck. The dog's eyes were filmy and opaque past the pain they conveyed. Rankin imagined them mirroring his own. He didn't know from them if the dog had in mind to rip his heart out. He had another vision of that woman in shadows, this time beckoning to him, as if trying to draw him into the darkness with her or maybe just deep enough into it for him to make out her face. With the forefinger and thumb of his free hand he seized the end of one of the quills protruding from the dog's snout; locking the animal's head between his other wrist and bicep, he yanked out the quill.

The dog made only a slight whimper. Rankin took hold of and jerked out another quill. The dog's body trembled, but it didn't fight Rankin. Rankin whispered to it, "Smart enough to know what's good for you." He felt drops of moisture on his face. He reached up and discovered the drops had come from his eyes. He swiped them away. He couldn't tell if it was the dog's or his own body trembling. He seized the end of a third quill and drew it out. He felt something loosen in him, as if one of his internal organs had come free of its moorings and was pushing its way up through his throat. He made a whimper like the dog's whimper. "There ain't no other way," he told it, "but to fucking hurt."

He yanked out another quill. He imagined the drone of an airplane traversing the space above them as a steel bit drilling into his skull. He felt himself being mystically drawn closer to the woman beckoning at him—now he saw her face angled downward, the sharp curve of her nose, the swell of her bosom. The dog's head positioned pliantly in his grip sudden-ly brought to his mind a shapeless life form he imagined he had spent his entire life struggling to at once rescue from itself and kill. "My mother made a great omelet," he told the dog.

He tugged a quill from the pulpy flesh of its nose. Drops of blood, sweat—maybe tears—rolled down the dog's face. Rankin dabbed more moisture from his cheeks. He sucked snot up into his nose.

He took from the dog all the quills in it (fifteen). He released the dog. The dog shook itself. Rankin took off his cap, dabbed lightly with it at the blood surrounding the gash on the animal's hip. Not deep, the cut nonetheless was vicious, as if made by a claw or fangs. He pulled up from the border sepa-rating the drive and bushes a half-frozen clump of grass and soil; he pressed the clump into the dog's wound, the dog squirming, though not protesting. "I ain't equipped to do no more for you," said Rankin.

The dog stood looking at him.

Rankin picked up his light and rose to his feet. A loud hee-haw shattered the night behind them. Rankin pivoted and looked toward the sound, seeing several hundred yards in the distance, through what looked to be woods, the shape of a dimly lit building. He turned back to the dog to try to convey to it that it should stay where it was, that in a few minutes Rankin would return for it, bring it back to his car, and put it in the hands of someone who would make it better and maybe even find it a permanent home.

The dog was gone.

Rankin turned away from the house he'd been headed for, angled his light at the ground before him, and started making his way toward where the hee-haw had sounded.

* * *

Little Charlie's mother, placing before Little Charlie a steaming concoction of eggs, toast, bacon, saying, "You're the only guy's ever loved me best for my omelets, Charlie."

In the algid air red oaks, elms, sugar maples, naked and bunched together, crackling, coated with hoarfrost. The underbrush thick with briers, nettles, Juneberry bushes. His light finally delineating a course moderately thinned by old pruning. Above ground roots like huge paralyzed snakes marring the path. A boulder he pictured a kid sitting next to a troll on. The sky's dim backdrop making of the overhead branches a spidery mosaic of twisted limbs. A dark winged shape silently piercing the canopy on its way into the woods. The hee-haw again, Rankin thinking how could anyone not know the source of that sound after hearing it once?

At the edge of the far side of the woods, he stopped.

He blinked, hoping the octagonal building a hundred-odd yards in front of him would vanish. It wouldn't. He crouched down. Past a vast open area he surmised to be lawn, the house showed three lights downstairs, one up. He could see in the driveway fronting the home, in a splash of light thrown from an entranceway lamp, the outline of a basketball hoop.

He remembered carving a person's name into a huge pine tree in those woods he'd run away into (not the name of anyone he knew) hoping a life attached to that name (it didn't matter whose life as long as it wasn't the life he'd been born to) would become his life. Shielding the light's bulb with his free hand, he stood and started for the house. In twenty-five or so yards he heard to his left what he took for a large animal moving about. He veered that way. Five or six steps brought him to a slatted wood fence. Keeping the beam on the ground, he played the light left and right. The fence looked to form a good-sized circle. Rankin had the sensation while gazing blindly into what he guessed to be a rounded paddock of being face to face with a creature described to him by a man who himself had not seen the creature, but had dreamed or imagined it. Then he remembered that in the dark dreams and imagination have better acuity than eyes do. A grey or brown animal, two-thirds the size of a horse, he told himself, with big floppy ears. He turned his back to the paddock.

He continued on his way to the house.

From the woods bordering the golf course an owl's sepulchral hoot reached him as the latest in a series of hoots. A moment later it occurred to him that he'd heard the earlier hoots in the series 24 hours ago, that this was the first hoot he'd heard out of those woods tonight.

The thought hit him that he, more than that creature he'd avoided seeing, ought to be locked away from the world.

His light beam exposed in the crystalline grass a muddied, roughed-up spot prompting him to picture a young boy rolling away from a man beating him with a shovel handle. In a few more steps he found the handle, splintered and dangling its spade.

He switched off the light and walked in an unwavering line to a flagstone patio on the house's near side; miniature statues and outdoor furniture (two chairs lay overturned) partially took up the space; a thick hemlock hedge lined its backside. The hedge ended at a concrete sidewalk, running, perpendicular to it, toward the driveway. In less than ten feet another walk turned sharply left off the main walk, directly to the house's front door. A lamp over the entranceway shadily illuminated the walk. Dark, moist blotches stained the concrete.

He strode down the walk to the stoop, the lamp limpidly displaying beneath him the stains. Similar, only larger, stains defaced the steps. A sickly odor tinged the air. He briefly stared, intrigued, at two small cannons, their barrels big enough to fit a hand into, framing the doorway. The stairway rail was sticky in his grasp. He had a vision of Florence in the flesh tied up back in the Tranny and of her soul next to him smoking a cigarette. He felt that woman in shadows pulling at him, as if he were a hunk of metal and she a magnet. He rang the doorbell. He reached to ring it a second time, then instead grasped and twisted the door handle.

The door was unlocked.

He pushed on it. Three-fourths of the way into the house the hardwood slab stopped moving with a dull thud that ended any hope Rankin had had that what he'd half-convinced himself he'd dreamed Little Charlie had done in that house last night Little Charlie hadn't done with Rankin wide awake.

He walked into the building and shut the door.

He peered down at the object that had halted it.

The dead guy's skin was pastier than Rankin remembered, the marks scarring his neck harsher, his blood darker, thicker (in places on him encrusted); his mouth, his nostrils, his eyes, staring fixedly at the ceiling, teemed with black flies; his broken-toothed expression might, in isolation, have been a grin or leer; the stink of him rotting added to the offal-and-piss stench as much a part of him as it was a part of the waste-permeated clothes half-torn from him.

Rankin felt vaguely sad and disappointed by the scene, a feeling similar to how he used to feel after flunking a grammar school test he knew he'd been smart enough to pass.

He recalled he'd been unable to picture the dead guy alive.

He tried to envision him living now—walking, talking, reading a book; still, he could picture him only as a mutilated, stinking corpse.

He picked up from the floor behind him a multi-colored throw rug and draped it over the body. The four foot rug covered the corpse only down to its knees.

He strode across the room, sat down on the lowest step of the stairs, picked up a walnut, opened it with his palms, dropped it in pieces at his feet. He gazed out at the upturned furniture, broken glass, smeared blood, scattered nuts, smashed telephone, festering human cadaver; as if it belonged to a person who had just come into the house and found him there, a voice inside him asked of him, Who was it that did this? Who is it that has come back to it?

Rankin picked up a pecan and randomly threw it toward the landing at the top of the open stairway right of him. The pecan hit a crystal chandelier hanging from the vaulted ceiling over the landing, scaring from the light an orange-and-black parrot. Watching the bird wing across the room, Rankin thought, it better not call me no names. It better not say to me a Goddamn thing.

The bird disappeared, squawking, down the far hallway.

Rankin gazed back up at the chandelier (transparent teardrops dangled from its bottom). Rankin couldn't remember having seen it before today, ever. He decided that must mean something; he couldn't say why or what it might mean. He speculated that living in a nice home like this one, knowing until you died no one could move you out of it, was about as good of a feeling as a person could have. He scooped up a handful of nuts, flipped them one at time at a large urn near the dead guy, trying to get them in the urn, recalling, as they hit the floor, the sound of falling pinecones landing at night on the floor of those woods he wished now more than ever he'd never left.

He stood, walked to and picked up the smashed telephone. He pressed its reset button, carried it over to and placed the lopsided instrument as best as he could make it fit into the cradle it had come out of. He looked back at the dead guy. He wondered what his name had been. He decided, whatever his name had been, the guy ought not to have to lie there half-exposed that way. He opened a closet left of the door, grabbed from it a man's raincoat, and lay it over the cadaver's calves and feet. He shoved the body against the wall. He put a table and two chairs in front of it. Then he followed on foot the parrot's earlier flight down the hallway.

He remembered finding in the laundry room of an apartment complex he and his mother were then living in a doctor's or nurse's smock (a very small person must have owned it because it was only a little big for Rankin, who couldn't have been more than eleven) and for a week or so walking around wearing the smock over his clothes, determined one day to be a doctor, to make sick people better.

He glanced into a room where six fish lay dead in a neat row on the floor, and, in a tank above them, a single bitten and chewed-on one moved in the perpetual motion that kept it alive. What sounded like a muffled cry or whisper reached him; he saw the parrot perched above the tank, flapping its wings. He wondered idly if this day had for him a tomorrow. He tried, but couldn't remember what had changed his mind about wanting to be a doctor; nor could he recall, after he'd stopped wanting to be one, ever again wanting to be something special or someone particular or wanting to be anything at all except big enough to not have to take anyone's shit. He heard from the room he was approaching a noise suggesting a muzzled dog trying to bark. The door to the room was three-quarters shut. He peered inside through the opening at a baby's crib, without, he remembered, a baby in it.

Or a baby was in it, making to him muted cries.

He pushed the door completely open.

In his head Florence's voice told him, "Don't dream it, Charlie."

The woman looked as if she'd fallen off the loveseat and been unable to right herself. She lay before the crib, partly on her back, partly on her left side, her mouth rhythmically opening and closing (Rankin recalled those green fish dying at his feet) emitting crackly, soft noises he was several seconds realizing were words.

He stepped into the room and over to her.

A folded, knotted scarf blindfolding her was darkly stained and moist, her bound wrists and ankles chafed and bleeding, the wine-colored fingerprints embedded in the flesh of her throat forming a brand to match the one on the dead guy. Rankin understood her to say, "Who's there?"

He leaned in at her.

"Hello?" the woman hissed.

Rankin knelt down next to her.

"Are you the police?"

Rankin shook his head. Then he recalled the woman couldn't see him. He said, "I maybe came to the wrong house."

The woman's lips stopped moving.

"I was looking for Maynard Cass's house."

The woman said nothing in reply. Rankin could feel her trying to draw a picture of him in her mind. He felt naked in the gaze of her thoughts. He said, "You thirsty?"

The woman's head moved in what he took for a nod.

"I'll get you some water."

The woman sibilated words he couldn't understand.

You idiot, thought Rankin. How could she drink water with

her hands tied? He reached down to her ankles and pulled at the cords securing them. The knots were tight. He couldn't loosen them. The woman's head rocked slowly side-to-side, bringing to his mind a set of windshield wipers in a rainstorm he had spent a long ride (he couldn't remember where or when) fixated on. "Swish, swish," a voice in his head reminded him. Rankin took out his gravity knife.

"He came back," the woman whispered.

Rankin threw out the knife blade. He imagined the woman flinching as it clicked open.

"He was ready to go—he was half out the door—and he came back—I was sure this time he would kill me for good—the hate, the anger—but then, then something in him—and he tied me tighter and, and, my eyes—"

Those eyes locating Little Charlie finally even behind his mask.

Rankin cut the cord from her ankles. Then he brought the knife up and severed the one securing her wrists. The woman seemed not to grasp that she was free. She lay still, moving only her hands, flexing them crab-like by her sides. For seconds, maybe minutes, she flexed them (they were bone-white and spotted purple). Rankin, avoiding looking at her blindfolded face, watched her fingers working in the air like the legs of two varmints being held up by the scruffs of their necks.

"He's at 210." The woman's haunted whisper might have been the scream of a person trapped deep within her. "The man you meant to see."

Rankin folded his knife.

"You're at 212."

Rankin slipped the knife into his pocket. He said, "I ain't got to see him right away."

The woman stiffened some. "He couldn't, could he, be here still?" Her question seemed to be directed not at Rankin, but to the wall past his head, a few feet below the ceiling.

Rankin wasn't sure who she was referring to; then he guessed she was referring to Little Charlie. "Nobody but me's here," he told her.

"And my husband. You've seen my husband?"

"I guess so. Somebody in the big room."

"My husband's dead. He killed my husband in front of me."

"Best you not think about that now."

"I tried to stop him." The woman's muted voice contained no inflection; she might have been reporting to Rankin the weather. "He was too strong."

"He was one person?"

"I didn't hear a heart in him, even when he was on top of me, killing me."

"A man alone?"

"He had no voice. No face."

"Not a boy?"

"A boy? A boy couldn't kill my husband. A boy couldn't do what he did to me." Rankin looked up from the woman's hands, at the tightly twisted scarf concealing her face above her nose. He couldn't remember, even in one of Little Charlie's dreams, anything happening in this room past when Little Charlie's mother's eyes had suddenly accused Little Charlie of causing everything.

Rankin stood up. "I'll be a minute fetching the water."

"I offered him what was in our safe."

"What?" said Rankin.

"He wouldn't even hear me. It didn't matter to him."

Rankin felt as if she was telling him about this guy he'd heard about but didn't know well, a guy she'd maybe gotten a handle on after spending time with and could fill him in on.

"What was he after if he wasn't after what you offered him?"

"To do just what he did do."

"What do you mean?"

"To torture us, to mutilate us. To murder my husband. To make me at once wish that he'd murdered me and grateful to him that he didn't." Rankin found the woman's matter of fact-ness, the monotonous cadence of her hollow whisper eerie, as if her voice were coming from a cassette deck playing inside her.

"Why would he pick out you and your husband to do that to?"

The woman moved painstakingly up into a half-sitting posi-tion against the loveseat. She'd made no motion to remove her blindfold. Nor had Rankin. Suddenly Rankin felt as if he were grasping at air while falling increasingly faster through it toward the ground. "I don't know," she said.

"Maybe it was a mistake."

"A mistake?"

A vision of the woman's eyes watching him independent of her hit Rankin. He suppressed a strong urge to get down on the floor and search under the furniture for them. "A guy don't do what he did without a reason."

The woman said in her crepitating voice, "I care less about him or his reasons than I care about a single bug being stepped on."

The thought struck Rankin that a criminal any good would have emptied the guy's safe, that someone who had done what had been done in this house and hadn't emptied the safe was-n't much of a criminal; Rankin wasn't sure what he was.

He walked from the room and down the hall toward the bathroom.

He remembered a doctor (the doctor's breath had smelled of peppermints) urging Little Charlie to tell the doctor the truth about how Little Charlie's face had gotten filled with the dozens of glass shards the doctor had just pulled with forceps from it, promising Little Charlie if he did tell the truth he'd be safe and bad things would never happen to him again, and

the doctor's disappointment (Little Charlie had felt like crying for how sad the doctor had seemed) when Little Charlie
had insisted to him he'd tripped and fallen face-first onto a
mustard bottle just like Little Charlie's mother had told the
doctor.

Specks of blood dotted the sink farthest from the bathroom
door. Rankin rinsed out the blood. He opened the medicine
cabinet above the sink. Why hadn't the woman, an internal
voice inquired of him, taken her blindfold off when Rankin
had freed her hands? Why hadn't Rankin taken it off for her?
Why was Rankin, as he stood there, suddenly petrified at the
thought of looking into the baby's crib? What didn't Rankin
remember happening last night just after, he remembered, the
woman's eyes had turned that way on Little Charlie? A sensation more horrible than the feeling of falling faster and faster
at the ground hit him; a sensation of falling at nothing, of
falling with no chance of landing.

He took from the cabinet a plastic cup and an aspirin bottle.

Even after Little Charlie had disappointed him, remembered Rankin, that doctor had given him a silver badge that
said on it, "I never cried."

He drew water into the cup. He brought it and the aspirin
bottle back to the woman. He fit the cup into her right hand.
The woman gripped the cup, though didn't seem aware of
doing so. "I haven't forgotten even a little bit."

"You'd maybe be better to," said Rankin.

She shook her head. "And I don't want to either. I'll be able
to help the police, even though I didn't see his face, with the
tiniest details." Her robe gaped somewhat at the top, partially
exposing her breasts to Rankin. Rankin wondered if she would
be more embarrassed if he told her about the break, if he
reached over and closed it, or if he said or did nothing and
later she discovered the robe had been open before him all that
while. Best, he thought, to ignore it. "He had a smoky, road-

weary smell. I imagined someone who'd spent a lot of time on buses and in crowded places, picking up other people's smells." She lifted the cup to her lips, her hand trembling, water dribbling onto her.

"His teeth were white—he couldn't have been a smoker, the smoke smell must have been from someone else—and straight. And horrible. Perfect teeth in a monster's mouth."

She sipped some water. She lowered the cup, moaning. "His nose was cut. Maybe it'll scar."

"Cut how?"

"I think my husband caused it."

She moaned again.

Rankin imagined that they were sharing the same pain, that they both hurt so bad everywhere that no part of them hurt the worst. He shook four tablets from the aspirin bottle; he put them in the woman's hand not holding the water glass. "What are they?"

"Aspirins."

The woman lowered her head silently at her palm.

"They were in your medicine cabinet."

"You're a doctor."

"No."

"A doctor or paramedic's on the way?"

"With the police."

"How long will they be? I don't want to forget things. I have a lot to tell them."

"They won't be long. You can tell me and when they get here I'll tell them whatever you don't."

The woman held the aspirins in her hand, facing Rankin. Rankin had a vision of two empty holes, where her eyes should have been, aimed at him. "He wore new boots."

"How do you know they were new?"

"They squeaked."

"Squeaked how?"

"When he walked." The woman swallowed wincingly. "I remembered them when I heard yours squeaking on your way toward me."

A painting on Buddha's cell wall of a guy strolling down a busy sidewalk, a black-and-white, bland figure in a crowd of fully fleshed-out people wearing bright colors, above the caption "A Dangerous Man."

"Where's the baby?" asked Rankin.

The woman's tongue, swollen and cracked, touched gingerly her lips, absorbing from them a single drop of water. "I don't know what you mean. There is no baby."

"There's a baby's crib in here."

"I was going to have a baby but last week I lost it."

"To who?"

"To God. He took it from me, after I'd carried it seven months."

"See the kinds of things He does? And people pray to Him."

"Did you call the police from the other room? Is that why I didn't hear you at it?"

Rankin touched the woman's hand holding the aspirins. "Best chew 'em 'fore you swallow 'em."

"Do what?"

"Shape a your throat it'll hurt less."

The woman moved her head slowly left, then right, as a seeing person would do to get their bearings upon waking in an unfamiliar setting. "Maybe I haven't been lying here alone as long as I thought," she whispered, again seemingly to some invisible person past Rankin. "Maybe he walked out of the room only a few minutes ago."

"You've been lying where you are a full day," said Rankin.

"How do you know how long I've been lying here?"

"From the looks of things."

The woman, appearing oblivious of doing so, let the aspirins roll from her palm into her lap.

"My girlfriend"—Rankin liked how it sounded, him saying he had a girlfriend—"she thinks I've got a good soul. That with her—another good soul—loving me I'll end up, after all the wrong I done, doing right."

"Doing right?"

"I'll know how, she says."

"Where is she?"

"My girlfriend?"

"Yes."

"She's in the car. I left her in my car."

The woman swallowed again. Rankin imagined her phlegm descending excruciatingly through her. She said, "You didn't, did you, give the police Maynard Cass's address? You told them two-twelve, not two-ten, Viner Lane?"

"You must be angry enough to kill," said Rankin.

"Angry?"

"I would be if I were you."

"There's a phone behind me, on the desk. You could call them again—to make sure you told them the right house."

"Angry enough at God to kill for what's been done to you."

"God didn't break into my house. God didn't murder my husband and all but murder me. A mute man in a mask did."

"He created the mute. Ain't He responsible for that?"

"For creating him maybe. Not for the life he chose to live."

"What would you know about that mute's life from your big golf course house life?"

The woman didn't answer. Suddenly exiting her more rapidly than it had been, air made a whistling sound in her nostrils. Rankin pictured a crowd of tiny people pushing and shoving to escape from her as if from a burning building.

"And He took your baby, who you'd have raised to a good life and He let Little Charlie be born to no life at all—how's that fair?"

The woman drank and spilled more water. She coughed up

some of what she'd half managed to swallow. "Did you tell them—the police"—she sputtered—"there's no number at the base of the drive? That we're the fifth house on the right after the club house?"

Rankin could tell she was hurt inside (bleeding from her guts, he guessed); he hurt in the exact way he imagined she did. "I'm sorry," he said.

"What?"

"That you're the one to take the brunt of it."

The water cup fell from the woman's hand to the floor.

"My girlfriend says anybody with a good soul would be happier locked up for life knowing they'd done right finally than running loose knowing they never had, but she ain't ever been locked up."

"You could ask her—your girlfriend—to stand at the bottom of the drive and flag down the police when they come."

"He didn't mean to do what he did to you. He mixed you up with someone else or he mixed up who he was with who he is. You see I'm confused, don't you?"

The woman didn't say.

"And that he can't be trusted?"

The woman tightly intertwined her fingers, then pushed them firmly into her lap as if implanting them in soil.

"That he'll turn on you in a heartbeat and what all he does after will be only a dream to Charlie Rankin?"

Little Charlie shoving his thumbs and index fingers into soft flesh, popping from their sockets, like snap peas from their shells, those eyes that wouldn't stop recognizing him.

"I ain't ate nothing all day," said Rankin.

He pulled the .22 from his belt.

"'Fore long it don't bother you not to." He watched the woman's hands shaking in her lap, her thighs quivering beneath her robe and felt as bad for her as he had for the deer he'd once accidentally run down with his car and then, sitting on the side of the road, watched slowly die. "If somebody put a steak in front of me now I'd sooner drop dead than eat it."

"I'm going to stand up," the woman whispered to the spot on the wall, "walk to the phone, call the police, and tell them what's happened here."

Rankin flicked off the .22's safety. "Can you have more babies?"

The woman's head moved mechanically up and down as if it were on a string being manipulated by an unseen hand.

"I wish I was the one you'd been carrying," said Rankin. "Then he'd never been born."

The woman's whole body was shaking. "You're going to have to help me."

"What?"

"Make it to my feet."

Rankin lay the .22 in her lap. "You ain't got to get to your feet."

"There is nothing you or Him or anyone," the woman told the wall in her toneless whisper, "can do to me anymore that frightens me."

"I don't want to frighten you."

"Help me up then. I can't make it up alone. He—I'm hurt too badly—can't you see that?"

Rankin picked up the woman's right hand and fit it around the gun and her index finger into the trigger guard. "You sit where you are. Save your strength." He placed her hand with the gun in it into her lap. "If you hear somebody after I leave walking at you through that door and not saying nothing"— Rankin tapped the woman's fingers on the gun—"aim this at the sound and pull the trigger and keep pulling it until you hear whoever it is fall and quit moving."

He got to his feet. "The safety's off. The clip's full."

The woman sounded to him at once as far away as a voice in a half-remembered dream and as near by as a mother nursing him. "Are you going to call them—the police—again?"

"I'm going to call them—I didn't before—from out in the big room," he told her, "and tell them exactly where to come and to come fast as hell and to bring with them an ambulance and to talk plenty loud on their way in here to rescue you."

"And then you're going to come back and wait for them with me?"

"That's the one part of it my girlfriend got wrong. That life inside ain't no life at all."

"They'll catch you. I'll make sure they do."

"Shoot me now, you'll know they will."

"Then you couldn't call them. And I'd likely die before a real human being found me."

Rankin started for the door.

"Why'd you come back?" the woman hissed at him.

Rankin quit walking. "To kill Maynard Cass," he said, not turning around.

"Why him? Why us, for God's sake?"

"I fucked up killing him last night by coming here instead. I musta counted houses wrong."

"All this—it was a mistake?"

Rankin wondered how Little Charlie last night, even with all they'd done to him, could have gotten enraged enough at his mother to take out her eyes. Hadn't she given him love? Hadn't she sung songs just to him? Hadn't she made him his own special omelets?

"William Pettigrew says there ain't no mistakes."

"I'd almost rather shoot you dead and die myself then let a monster like you walk away." The woman, cradling the gun atop her legs, refaced the wall; she whispered to it, "And I don't forgive you—not in this lifetime."

"Neither do I," said Rankin.

* * *

He told the 911 dispatcher he and a kid named Charlie had committed the carnage the police would find in the house when they arrived, but that Rankin was mostly to blame for it because he'd brought the kid there knowing the kid had a history in tight spots of getting all mixed up and going off on strangers to him as if they weren't strangers to him and things last night had gotten that kind of tight and the kid had gone off on these people something awful.

"Where's Charlie now?"

"You ain't got to worry about that."

"Why don't I have to worry about it?"

"I got him under control. He won't hurt nobody else."

"He's still there—in the house?"

"He's someplace you'll never find him at. Don't waste your time on it."

"Okay. Fine. We'll come back to Charlie. The lady though—she's breathing all right? She's okay?"

"She won't be you don't get somebody here quick."

"A squad car and an ambulance are about set to leave here. They'll be to you in fifteen, twenty minutes tops. Now, the man—"

"Forget him."

"No chance, at all, he isn't dead? You checked for vital signs?"

"Just tell them—the ones coming—the fifth house on the right after the golf course road."

"I got that. I wrote it down already."

"There'll be a Trans Am parked a few yards up the drive and a woman tied up in it."

"The injured woman?"

"No. Another woman. My girlfriend. She ain't a part of this."

"Does she need medical assistance?"

"She needs to be untied is all. She's my girlfriend."

"You said that. But you didn't say why she's tied up."

"I didn't want her seeing this."

"Seeing what."

"These people. What he did to them. She thinks she could handle knowing him but she couldn't."

"I'll make sure they—the officers—know to look for her."

"Just remember she had nothing to do with it. She's the one got me back here tonight."

"Okay."

"If not for her I wouldn't be on the phone with you now. I wouldn't be in this house again—understand?"

"I understand. So tell me about you—what can I call you first off? What's your name?"

"Don't even bother with that shit."

"It's just easier knowing who I'm talking to, that's all. I'm Ed."

"That don't matter a shit to me. Tell them, when they get here, to look straight off in the baby's crib for the woman's eyes."

"Did you say for them to look for her eyes?"

"Maybe the doctors can put them back in their sockets— like how they can sew peoples fingers back on their hands—let her see again."

"Did someone—Christ—did one of you—what are you telling me?"

"I remember him staring into the crib, thinking what happened to the baby?—then her eyes turning on him that way and him thinking no you don't blame me for it—then I find her tonight in a blindfold and neither of us wanting to take it off and me feeling afraid to look in the crib from a terrible feeling I know what's in it."

The dispatcher cleared his throat. "Charlie did this? You're telling me that Charlie—he did what exactly?"

Rankin didn't say anything.

The dispatcher cleared his throat again. "Is there a baby in that house?"

"No."

"You mentioned a baby's crib."

"It never got born."

"So in the house right now is just you, the dead man, and the injured woman?"

"Right."

"No baby."

"I got from what she said she lost it a good while 'fore all this happened to her."

"And no Charlie."

"I'm hanging up now."

"Wait, now just—you'll be there when they—the officers and medical personnel—arrive?"

"I know it won't mean nothing much to anybody but I'm sorry as hell for what Charlie and me done here."

"We don't want any trouble, is all. We just want to help who's injured, right?"

"Right."

"You're not armed?"

"I ain't armed."

Rankin hung up the phone.

He strode down the hallway to the room containing the crib and, saying nothing, entered the room and made straight for the woman. The first bullet got him in the right shoulder blade. The next one in the belly, above his belt. He sagged forward, still moving. Two bullets entered the wall left of him; he heard another one splinter the ceiling, before a stinging sensation in his chest right of his heart took away his wind. He fell to his knees, even as he realized he'd been shot in one of them. He crawled ahead. A bullet hit him in the Adam's apple. He collapsed onto his belly and slithered at the woman. Her blindfold was off and she was eyeing him down the .22's barrel and Rankin tried to laugh from joy upon discovering that Little Charlie had had enough good left inside of him to spare his poor mother her sight, but only a gasp came out of him. He stopped moving inches from the woman's feet. She dropped the gun. He heard her whisper at the wall or at him, "Now, we'll wait."

About the Author

Matthew F. Jones is the author of the novels *Deepwater, The Elements of Hitting, A Single Shot, Blind Pursuit,* and *The Cooter Farm,* each critically acclaimed. His novel *Deepwater,* named by critics as one of the best novels of 1999, has recently been made into a film starring Lucas Black, Peter Coyote and Lesley Ann Warren. Jones was born in Boston and raised in rural upstate New York. He lives with his family in Charlottesville, Virginia.